Double Fight

Trista Bergstrom

WestBow Press books may be ordered through booksellers or by contacting:

WestBow Press
A Division of Thomas Nelson & Zondervan
1663 Liberty Drive
Bloomington, IN 47403
www.westbowpress.com
844-714-3454

ISBN: 979-8-3850-3532-8 (sc)
ISBN: 979-8-3850-3533-5 (e)

Library of Congress Control Number: 2024920935

Print information available on the last page.

WestBow Press rev. date: 10/18/2024

Contents

One

Jordan Lawson lived a boring life. Bouncing around from town to town, not really having many friends, until she met Mike Dawson in the seventh grade. They had been attached at the hip ever since. They had moved to this little town.

They did everything together. They had all of their classes together, they went on field trips together and they only lived a couple blocks away from each other. And if they weren't at one house, they were at the others.

He had been the rock in her life ever since then, everyday. She had been the awkward new girl in the school. She had ugly cheap second hand clothes and big plastic glasses. She had been the only girl raised with her brother by their father. She was average height, about five feet five inches, and about 120 pounds. Even though she was awkward, all the girls thought she was awesome! She had long blonde hair and deep blue eyes. She had the hottest best friend in the whole school and she could kick anyone's but that she wanted, if she wanted.

Her father was a very smart man, and he was a black belt and had been training with her and her brother ever since she could remember.

Her mother was someone they never really talked about. She had died when she was born and they hadn't talked about her much since. When Jordan was a little girl, she would often ask questions and her father would get distant and upset and so she soon learned after a little help from her brother that her father would be much happier if they never talked about her again. Not that she was religious but she liked to think that someone was watching over her.

From the moment they met, they knew that they had a bond. Not that they loved each other right away or some fluffy crap of love at first sight. But they knew that they would forever be a part of each other's lives. They were always together, from then on moving forward in their lives. She had always prayed for her father to be happy, now she prayed that her father didn't move them again.

They went through middle school as best friends and she never once thought that she needed other friends. She hung out once in a while with some of the girls, but none that would call them her best friends forever. And she didn't either. She knew who her friend was and that would never change.

Two

He was a part of her life and was not threatened by her knowledge and skills in Taekwondo. They had a lot of fun training together. As an athlete, he was built well enough to take a good hit and still get up (because she knocked him down a lot!) He was a good sport and always encouraged her.

Michael had been her friend and a confidant in a new place, and a training partner when her brother was too busy starting high school and a confidant when she needed someone to keep a secret. He wasn't sure when it happened, or if it had happened for him over time, or if it had somehow been there since the day they met. However, when he realized it, he tried to not ever show it to her that his feelings had changed. They hung out and had pizza and watched movies, played board games and when they were working out, he took the hits and gave some back even harder to hide his frustration from his feelings about her.

When they hit eleventh grade, he began to see that he may not be able to hide his feelings for her for much longer. He didn't know what to say. One day they were sparring and she was kicking his butt. As Jordan threw a jab with a very well placed round kick that he totally should have been able to block, he went down like a ton of bricks. Jordan took off her helmet and asked, "What's up? You should have seen that coming a mile away!" "Sorry I just got some things on my mind." He replied.

"Don't apologize to me, you are the one that has to go home with bruises." She snorted.

Sparked by her snarkyness, he responded with, "Maybe you should just come over and here and nurse me back to health!" And with that gave her a little tug on her arm.

She felt the spark between them and it startled her and she jumped back and said, "Hey I forgot that my dad wants me home early for dinner tonight and I have a lot of homework to get done, I better get to it." And she left with a little wave!

"Yea, ok. See you tomorrow." He replied, and he watched her grab her bag and walk away. He didn't know what he thought she would say, or even if she even had an inkling of the same types of feelings. What had he expected? That she would jump into his arms and kiss him like he had dreamed she would. He knew that was a naïve thought to say the least. He angrily grabbed his bag and started walking home.

The next few days they kept a bit of a distance from each other, never admitting that anything had happened. He asked her two days later if they were going to work out after school and she nodded. They met at the gym after seventh period and began to stretch. Jordan started talking about school and the regular stuff and their relationship seemed normal again. They worked out and Michael seemed to have his head in the game today and he had his head in the game and was able to not only defend himself but add a few hits that Jordan didn't see coming.

They had a very thorough workout and seemed to fall back into place. They were taking a water break when he blurted it out, "I'm sorry about the other day, I just can't hold it in anymore. I see you everyday and I want to be more a part of your life!" He put his hands on her shoulders and he put his lips on hers and kissed her. He saw a look on her face that he had never seen before, and he pulled away. The look of someone who had been slapped in the face, and Jordan having the skills that she had, is something that had never happened to her before.

Tears started to come down her face and she didn't say anything. She didn't know what to say, or how to say it. She wasn't one to cry, ever. Even the thought of crying made her mad and she tried to control it and the more she tried to control it the more she lost control. He still had his arms on her shoulders and he looked at her with his stunning blue eyes and said "Why are you crying?" She still couldn't speak and she got madder that she was still crying and she backed up, grabbed her bag and ran.

Wow! Had he envisioned this ending differently? She was amazing, and he had made her cry by the mere thought that he would want something more from their relationship. Was he so terrible?

Jordan ran to the locker room. She knew that most of the sports were still practicing and the locker room should be fairly empty, so no one would see her crying. She threw her bag on the bench and collapsed against a locker. Now, being away from him she seemed to be able to gain some control. Around him she couldn't seem to control herself. She found that when around him, she felt secure and safe. She found herself wanting to stay in his arms when he happened to get a lock on her and never move. Her competitive spirit soared to life on those occasions and she ended up getting out of the lock and then regretting it a moment later when she turned around to look at him. She couldn't figure out what had just happened up there. She was stupid to think that it wouldn't eventually happen. Even when her father had set her down to have the incredibly awkward conversation of the birds and the bees, the thought had crossed her mind of being with Mike eventually, she just didn't think that he would have the same feelings.

Amid her thoughts she never heard the footsteps of Kate who was the female version of Mike. She played many varsity sports when she was a freshman and both her Mike could probably out play most seniors at almost any sport. This is who Jordan thought that Mike would end up with. "What's wrong with you? You get thrown to the mats finally by Mike?" she asked.

Jordan replied with her own attitude as though she had never missed a beat, "Not on his best day!" Jordan felt her own strength and wit coming back to her and she stood up to show that she was fine.

"So what has all your panties in a bunch? I didn't think anything would ever break you down." Kate said.

"I could say the same to you." Jordan replied.

Kate responded with a slight smile. Realizing that she had found an opponent who wasn't afraid to challenge her, she started to walk out of the locker room. She turned on her heel and said, "Hey, if you ever want to blow off some steam, I am always up for a good run. Give me a call."

Jordan didn't know what to think so she smiled back and said, "Only if you try to keep up."

Jordan didn't know what to do about Mike, so for now she decided not to do anything until something came to her that would lead her in the direction of what to do. She was terrified to admit her feelings to him. What happens if it didn't work? She had watched her father in relationship after relationship and clearly they never worked out, so that was the only frame of reference she had to go off of. Relationships never work out, so why ruin the best friendship that she had for a relationship that was doomed from the beginning. So she grabbed her bag and walked out of the locker room to go home.

Three

Jordan and Kate began to run every day. They met up at five in the morning and ran at least five miles. Kate loved to run, but Jordan had something to run from. She tried not to think about Mike. Over the past couple weeks, they hadn't talked much. Jordan had been distant and Mike looked angry every time she looked at him.

Kate knew that something was wrong with Jordan and Mike's friendship; however she didn't feel that she and Jordan had crossed the bridge of being able to ask that question yet. But she was bolder than most people, so she went for it; "So are you ever going to tell me what Mike did that has you two lovebirds fighting?"

"We are not lovebirds!" Jordan huffed exhausted and out of breath from running.

"Ok, so the fact that you deny it means that just because it hasn't happened yet, doesn't mean that it won't. And because that was the first thing you deny says that your little spat has something to do with that!" Kate retorted.

Jordan knew that she was right and although she didn't want to admit it and still refused to, she said, "nothing happened, just we seem to be growing apart. See you at school." And she ran to her house to get ready for school.

Kate decided that she enjoyed her new running partner more than she enjoyed idle gossip, so she let it go and headed to her house to get ready for school too.

While at school Jordan and Mike had gotten pretty good at avoiding each other, however today he walked straight up to her and said, "Hi."

Kate, standing next to Jordan, decided that she would head to class, "Well that's my cue" and she turned and walked away. Jordan looked at Mike and she felt that her stomach became a bottomless pit and her oatmeal breakfast was soaring to the bottom. She looked up to Mike in his beautiful blue eyes and prayed that he wouldn't say anything about the last time they were together.

He looked at her, "Well it looks like you and Kate are getting along well."

Jordan seemed to come out of her trance when she didn't look at him, so she looked at the floor and replied, "yea we have been running together, she keeps me on my toes."

"That's good. Have you been working out?" he asked.

"Only with my father, but he tends to go easy on me. He thinks that he is going to hurt me." She said, again looking at the floor.

"Well, if you want a real workout I will be at the gym after class." He saw the apprehension on her face and he replied to it with, "just a work out I promise." He smiled and walked away.

She wasn't sure what to think, but she needed the workout. So as she walked to class, she decided that the reason that she didn't want to really admit her feelings was to not lose her friend. So she might as well go and hang out with her friend doing the things that had made them friends. Otherwise, what was the point?

While she and Kate were changing in the locker rooms after class, Kate was eyeing her new friend suspiciously. "So you haven't worked out with him in a few weeks."

Jordan looked up at her and raised an eyebrow, "and…" she replied.

Kate shrugged, "Just an observation, you seem to have been avoiding him and now you aren't."

Jordan looked at the floor again, "I need the workout, I have to practice my taekwondo or my skills won't be up to par. He is a good partner."

Kate started to walk out and with a sly smile she said, "I bet he is."

Jordan chuckled and rolled her eyes. Kate was always good for a laugh or a good joke. You could always count on her to have her mind in the gutter.

The workout went not so well. Jordan had been trying to land a 360 sidekick. And that was all she focused on. Every time her mind drifted to those super sweaty hot tense muscles on Mike's body, she lost focus and fell down and it hurt. She tried to focus, she could not figure out how he could be so composed. After all he was the one who had confessed his feelings, not her. She should be the one who was calm and him all tied up in knots. She fell several more times with these thoughts in her head. She was not getting it. It was getting late and she had a lot of homework to get done. She figured that with the way her concentration was going, she better get started. "Well I better get going; I have a lot of homework to get started." She told him.

"Yea me to. I have to get started on that Shakespeare essay." Mike responded. There was an awkward moment and then he turned and grabbed his bag and said, "See ya tomorrow Kicks." "Kicks" was a nickname he had given her when they were in middle school and they had started working out together. She had a killer round kick and her kicks were far stronger than her punches. She smiled at the familiar nickname and watched him leave.

As she was leaving school she found Kate waiting at the entrance for her. Since they lived on the same block, they had been walking home together and chatting and becoming friends. They had known each other since Jordan had moved here, but never been particularly fond of each other. Kate smiled when she saw how Jordan was wincing while touching her shoulder. It was the shoulder she had fallen on several times while not paying attention. Jordan realized why Kate was smiling and she smiled back, while adding a "shut up!" in there.

Kate and Jordan chatted about how their practices went. They reached their houses and said goodbye.

Jordan turned into her driveway and walked up to her house dreading the countless hours of homework ahead of her.

Homework was going ok when her dad called her for dinner. Which was a laughable thing anyway, her dad could barely make macaroni and cheese, usually it was ordering out for pizza. So dinner that was cooked at home tended to be something of an adventure. She came down stairs and her brother and father were sitting at the table with a box of pizza. She grabbed a plate and threw a couple of slices on it. Her dad asked how school was going. Her brother launched into how football practice was going and their upcoming game against the Bulldogs and how they intended to crush them. As he went on about the tight ends and defense ability, Jordan's thoughts drifted to her workout. Her father would certainly have some sort of exercise to get her mind on her training, if he knew that she didn't have her mind completely focused. She certainly didn't want that kind of exercise today. She focused her attention on her brother. She apparently wasn't paying as much attention to him as she thought she was. She vaguely heard her father say her name and said, "huh" as a response.

Her father raised an eyebrow at her, "Where has Mike been? Usually he would have been here for supper three times this week already."

"Oh he has been working on his Shakespeare essay a lot lately." Jordan responded quickly.

"That's good he is focusing on school and his sports and not just being your punching bag. I see you have been running with a girl from school lately. That will help with your cardio and endurance." Her father observed.

Her brother watched this conversation go on with interest, and then as usual with her brother Josh, he had to get his two cents in, "About time that she started hanging out with a girl." While saying this, he gave her a playful nudge on the shoulder. However her mood lately had been anything except playful. She grabbed his wrist, twisted it and leaned in on his shoulder which pushed his face to the table.

"You may be a belt ahead of me big brother but I can still kick your butt!" She said; her father watched this exchange without flinching. He thought that the competition to keep them on their toes was a good thing. He was always talking about being on their guard. As far as raw skill went, she had more of it than he did. Being two years older and having more experience doing it than she did, he should be better than her. But she caught on to things far faster than he did. Josh had always wanted to do taekwondo; he just didn't have the passion for it that Jordan did. And like she said, she was better than him.

Their family had been a rough house family her whole life. Always punching and kicking each other, not to be mean, but in the rough housing loving family kind of way. Both having been trained in the martial arts their whole lives, they knew what would really cause damage and how far they could go. She let her brother go and sat back down to finish her pizza. "Geez Kicks chill out!" Josh said. Obviously the nickname had stuck to the whole family.

Jordan rolled her eyes as her father and brother went back into football talk. She thought about her homework and began to gobble up her pizza so she could get back to it. Unlike Mike, she had finished her Shakespeare essay; however she did have other tests to study for. She excused herself from the table with the excuse of an algebra test to study for. When she got to her room she sat in her chair and grabbed her algebra book and opened it up to chapter six and began to work on her pretest. She managed to concentrate for two hours before she decided to go take a shower and go to bed.

She fell asleep fast after all of her training and running today. She saw his face in and out of her dreams. She felt his hands on her and he leaned in.... then she jumped awake. Her heart was racing and she was shaking. She didn't remember what she was dreaming about, or why she was so worked up. But she knew it had to be about her somewhat of an argument with Mike. She lay back down on her pillow and tried to think about something else to try to get herself back to sleep. She thought about her kick that she was having trouble with, nope, that only seemed to frustrate her. So she tried to think about her algebra. Trying to solve for X ......that did the trick she was fast asleep again.

Four

The chiming went on over and over in her head and she couldn't make it stop. Then she realized that it wasn't in her head, it was her alarm clock. She reached over and shut it off. She crawled out of bed and grabbed her running clothes and put them on. She was usually bright and chipper in the mornings, however, this morning she was not feeling up to life. She assumed that it was due to her dreams, whatever it was about. She put her hood up and went outside to meet Kate. They met on the corner and stretched. Kate, although she loved to run, hated early mornings. So she whined a bit about how she wanted to sleep in and Jordan smiled, she loved nothing more than running while the sun came up, then Jordan started the play list and they got going. They ran and ran until they had run for 5 miles and ended up back at their block. When they got back Kate stopped and put her hands on her knees and Jordan leaned up against a tree. Kate looked at Jordan and said, "You were kind of lagging today. Usually you have a couple steps ahead of me."

Jordan stared at her and that was when she decided to trust Kate. "I think I was having some dreams. I don't really remember what they were about, but I clearly didn't sleep well."

Kate studied her and said "People usually have dreams based on the things going on in our lives and the dreams are supposed to help us work through our issues."

Jordan didn't know how to respond to that. "I know I have issues with some things, but how are my dreams supposed to help me work through them if I don't remember them?"

Kate shrugged and laughed, "Pick you up in thirty for school."

Jordan went home and got showered and was finishing her oatmeal when she heard Kate honk the horn. She grabbed her backpack and took off out the door. They got to school in no time and were walking to class, when Kate said, "So you can't remember your dreams to help you through your issues, but you know that I read Cosmo every month and so I am sure that there has been an article on what you are going through that I might remember. I mean I am just saying, "you aren't a good running partner if you are not challenging me."

Jordan chuckled at Kate and said "Well the usual stuff of teen drama you know."

Kate said "No, teen drama is a B in algebra, English term paper, and boy drama. You are a straight A student, we don't have any term papers due, and the only boy drama you could have is with Mike and since you were training with him yesterday; I dare say that is fine."

Suddenly Kate saw the pain on Jordan's face and she knew this was serious. "He kissed me." She stated flatly.

Kate put her arm around Jordan and said, "Jordan, you could do worse! He is gorgeous and smart and you two were meant for each other."

Jordan said "And if not, we ruin a friendship that has been there forever."

Kate looked at her "And because of that friendship you could have the best relationship ever. And if you are right, and it doesn't last and your friendship doesn't survive, then it wasn't real to begin with. That's the bell, I have to go. Think it over."

Jordan watched her friend walk away. At the end of the hallway, she saw Mike. Their eyes met, and he gave her his usual friendly wave and smiled and walked into class. Jordan smiled at her two friends and she walked to class thinking about what Kate had said. Even though Mike and she had only been friends for years, they both felt that they had always been a part of each other's lives forever. It was important to her that the friendship with Mike stays intact. She felt that if her friendship with Mike ended a piece of her would go with it. It wasn't anything she wanted to find out. On the other hand, Kate had a point. Their fictional relationship could be epic! On the other hand, how to go about it and did she want to take the chance. Or she could do the algebra test that was in front of her, she wasn't sure which prospect was more daunting!

She walked out of algebra feeling like she had run ten miles. Mentally exhausted and physically drained. She caught up to Kate at their lockers, Kate took one look at her and said "good grief girl! I would have thought that you went ten rounds with Mike Tyson, but I really know what Mike you were wrestling with!"

Jordan smirked, "Mr. Smith's algebra test. I feel like I went ten rounds with Mike Tyson. I think my brain is mush. If I never see another X versus Y equation, it will be too soon! I am trying not to think of the other Mike."

"I hear my name and I am here to serve!" said Mike behind Jordan.

Jordan almost jumped out of her skin. "What? Oh, hi! We were just talking about Mike Tyson!"

Kate giggled "Have you taken the algebra test yet? Jordan just got done and she said it was killer."

Mike looked from Jordan to Kate "I took it first period, it was rough. Hey are you ready to hit the pads?" he said glancing at back to Jordan.

Jordan glanced at Kate, "Yea, let me go change. I need the workout and then maybe I will sleep better tonight!"

This time, Jordan was focused and landed all kicks on target, and she didn't think once about the kiss. It was nice to feel like she was one hundred percent. Mike took the hits like a champ. He made her work for it, and she launched herself into the mechanics of each kick and hitting every single one on the money. Her father would be proud. This is partly why she didn't work out with him too much anymore. He was always proud, but instead of just being proud, he would raise the bar. She was also grateful for that, he pushed her to be the best that she could possibly be. However, sometimes it was nice to not have to be perfect. They finished the workout and Jordan felt great!

She said that she better hit the showers and head home to get some homework done and try to get a good night's sleep. Mike just smiled at her. She turned and started walking out feeling like her world was falling back into place. She could feel his eyes lingering on her, so before she even realized she was doing it, she was adding a little swish to her step. She got showered and changed and grabbed her backpack and gym bag and headed out of the gym.

Five

Jordan felt groggy for some reason. She felt like she was hung over, even though she had never been drunk, but if she had she figured that this is what it might feel like. She is trying to figure out why she felt like this. She can't remember going home or doing homework and this didn't feel like her bed, and she felt something around her wrist but she couldn't place what it was. She wanted to know what was going on; to know what to expect before she opened her eyes, because something about this felt all wrong. She felt weird all around; she just couldn't quite get her head around things to understand what was happening, so she opened her eyes. Nothing she saw filled her with anything but absolute terror all the way to the tips of her toes.

Jordan could feel the tears coming down her face, but no sounds were coming out. She could see the stone all around her. And she could feel her wrists and ankles inside the metal holding her down.

She didn't know what happened or what was going on, other than everything was terribly wrong. She fell asleep crying.

When she woke up the next time, she was unshackled and there was a plate with a sandwich and carrots next to the lamp. She didn't know if she should eat it or not. She looked around, freaked out, she didn't know where she was or why. But all she could see was a giant wooden door, with a little peep window in it. Other than that, there were stone blocks on the wall and the floor was concrete. There was no getting out!

Six

Kate was at home at her desk in her room working on her English paper when her phone rang. It was Jordan's dad, "Hello Brad. No, I haven't seen Jordan since Algebra this afternoon. I think she went to the gym with Mike. Of course I will let you know if I see her. Has she not come home yet? Have you talked to Mike? Please let me know."

Kate wasn't really worried. Jordan and Mike have worked out late before. It wasn't abnormal for them to not hear their cell phones. Kate refocused on her homework and tried to finish. An hour later, her phone rang again. It was Mike this time. "Hey Mike, did you and Jordan finally finish pounding each other to pulp?"

"Kate, I am a little worried. Jordan and I finished working out around five thirty this evening. She went to shower and change and I haven't seen her since." Mike replied.

"So are you telling me that you haven't seen her since the shower....?" Kate snooped.

"God Kate is that all you think about? And no, I saw her in the gym, I didn't follow her to the shower." Mike responded with exasperation.

Kate came to attention and started putting the pieces together. "Wait, have you talked to Brad?"

"Yea, five minutes ago. He still hasn't seen her." Mike said.

"Um, ok. I am trying not to freak out here because that was like three hours ago and nobody has seen her. Where would she go? Has she ever done anything like this before?" Kate asked with a very high note of tension in her voice and a twinge of guilt. She brushed it off earlier and she should have been worried, maybe even starting to look somewhere or do something.

Mike sounded worried too when he responded, "no she has always been with one of us; Josh, Brad, or myself. Oddly, one of the most capable women I know has always been surrounded by men, and the one time she isn't we all lose our minds."

"So Mike, what do we do?" Kate said.

"Well, Josh and Brad are at their house right now, probably going nuts. So I think that I am going to head over there and see if I can calm things down or if they have heard anything."

"Do you think that I should go too?"

Mike responded, "I don't think that will help. I can tell you are freaking out, and I think that your nerves may only feed theirs. So if you can calm your nerves and act like you're not freaking out, then yes stop over."

"Ok yea, I can act. See you there." Kate responded.

Kate walked calmly and slowly up to the house. She had never actually walked to this house. She didn't drive because she knew that she wouldn't be able to calm herself and be able to present the attitude that she would need to have when she went in there if she only had the couple minute drive over here. She had only ever driven or ran. Running obviously wouldn't do either. So she had chosen to walk. She casually strode up to the door and Mike must have seen her walking so he opened the door before she even had to knock. She walked in and saw Josh and Brad on the couch and she took a breath and walked in and said "hey guys."

Josh looked up and smiled but Brad seemed to be in a different world. "Hey Kate, have you heard anything from Jordan?"

"No, but I am sure that nothing is wrong. She probably went to the library and is studying. I know she has been working on some English stuff." Kate responded. She thought that it was rather nonchalantly. She was rather proud of herself so she added in, "do you have any chips? I have the munchies." Josh smiled, nodded, and pointed to the kitchen.

Mike followed her and now that she had food in her hands, and she was at Jordan's house, she was calming down. She looked at him and quietly asked, "Ok so we know that she isn't at the library, so now what."

Mike responded, "Brad called the police and they said they can't do anything for twenty-four hours, and since I last saw her at six; that puts the clock at eighteen hours left."

Kate got a weird look on her face and said, "Earlier you said you saw her at five-thirty?"

"No it was six, you must have mis-heard." Mike said, turning to the sink.

"Ugh, no, I don't mess up details!" Kate said and absolutely exasperated.

"Well then maybe I just mis-spoke. Whatever the time was, the cops won't do anything yet, so we just have to go look for ourselves." Mike responded.

"Hold on, what's going on here?" Kate asked.

"What do you mean? We are trying to find out what's going on with Jordan" Mike said a little nervously and walked back to the living room.

Kate tended to have a sixth sense about underlying things that people didn't want to other people to know. But somehow she knew, when someone was holding something back, and she sensed it now in Mike. Kate followed him, with the chips.

They got back to the living room to Josh being mad about not being able to go out and start looking. "You don't even know where to start looking!" Brad said to him.

"So what are we supposed to do, just sit here and do nothing?" Josh yelled.

Brad stopped looking at the floor and looked at his son. "I know that it's hard. But we have to be strong. She is a strong, capable woman. There isn't much that could happen to her that she couldn't handle. I am sure that she is fine, just not entirely sure where she is exactly."

Mike decided to jump in, "I will drive him around and we will see what we can find." Josh looked at him like he had just handed him a million dollars. They grabbed their sweatshirts and walked out the door.

Kate hollered after them, "I will stay here with Brad, and the chips. Brad, do you want anything to drink?" She was pretty sure he didn't hear her, so she flopped down on the couch and turned on the TV. It was over an hour later and they hadn't heard anything, so Kate told Brad that she would text Mike to see if they found her. She got his text back saying that they hadn't seen anything but they would check the Dairy Queen, and bring her the Oreo blizzard that she wanted. She could see Mike's eyes rolling through the text. She didn't really want to tell Brad that they hadn't found anything, so she said that they were going to check the Dairy Queen. After another hour, she texted him again and said, "Soooooo????" Ten minutes later and a lot of pacing, she got his text back. "Headed back." There was something about that text that made her think they found a body and she was about to have a panic attack so she told Brad she was going to head to the bathroom. She got to the bathroom and started breathing like she was going to cry. She sat down and decided that she wasn't going to cry, if she cried then she would not be able to stop. So she stood up and looked in the mirror and told herself "Stop! You don't get to breakdown now. They need you to be strong." She took a deep breath in and opened the door. When she stepped into the living room, she saw the car pull up that the boys were in and then behind it, a cop car.

The boys came in with the officers. Brad looked up at them and you could see his world crash in his face as he realized that something was drastically wrong. Josh sat down beside his father and started to tell the story that they were looking and decided to try to retrace her steps. They went to the school and walked from the locker room to the stairs and up and out the door. Around the corner is the parking lot and while looking around, Mike noticed something under one of the cars. When they went over to take a closer look, Mike couldn't touch it and it took him a long time to stand up. He finally did, and he told Josh that it was Jordan's gym bag. They called the police and they found a cloth that the police believe may have chloroform on it. After telling the story, he waited for a reaction from his father. He started shaking his head and then you could see the tears start and Kate ran over to him and hugged him. The police told Brad that they were opening an investigation and they would keep the family informed. They all stayed on the couch overnight. When the sun rose in the morning, no one knew what to do. How do you go on? Or do you go on? Do you just wait?

Seven

Jordan didn't know what to say, or if she should say anything. He looked at her and said, "Eat. You will need your strength. There are rules here. " Jordan didn't know what to do. She was shaking all over. "I said, 'Eat'. Now for the rules. You need to eat to keep up your strength. I have written down things for you to do while you are here. You need not scream, no one will hear you. It is just easier if you don't do it."

"You will have workouts every day. During those workouts, you will be guarded and there is no sense trying to escape."

"Why am I here?" Jordan could barely get the words out.

"Well you will soon understand the reason. But essentially, you were brought here for entertainment." He said.

"Entertainment? What kind of entertainment?" Jordan asked.

"Well, you will soon find that out!" Like I said, no yelling, and you need to get your workouts in. And eat your food." He said.

"Is there anyone other than me here?" Jordan asked.

"Now, you don't need all of the information. You will find out everything else soon enough."

Eight

Mike and Kate got up and made some breakfast for Josh and Brad, which of course they not only didn't eat, but didn't even look at it. They called the officer for any updates and were told that they still did not have any new information. This did not help anything at all. Brad told the three kids that they should go to school, maybe they will be able to talk to their friends and be able to see if anyone knows anything. Or maybe they will find someone who saw something. Josh isn't keen on the idea of letting Brad be home by himself. However, Mike talked Josh into it and the three of them left. They agreed to run by Kate's house for her to pick up her bag and some new clothes.

They got to school and when they walked in, it was like they were on the red carpet. The crowds parted for them and the people stopped talking. Kate, who was between the two guys, looked at both of them and asked "which one of you two decided that this was a great idea?"

A couple of concerned friends stopped and asked what the story was, or if they had heard anything new. Most people were too afraid to talk to Josh, but some people were brave enough to ask Kate, because they knew that she was usually pretty outspoken and somewhat of a new friend of Jordan's. Kate told them that they didn't know anything, and nothing had been substantiated. So basically, they knew nothing!

After a while, Kate couldn't remember how many times she had said this. After the third day of this, she was getting really mad. "Mike, I swear, the next person to ask me if I know anything new is going to get their head bit off!"

Mike looked at her and gave her a small smile. "Hang in there Kate, people are just worried."

"How are you doing?" Kate asked him. He shrugged in response. "Mike, please take care of yourself. Make sure that you are eating and sleeping. You can't just spend your days at school and nights with Brad and Josh and taking care of everyone else."

"I promise I will take care of myself." Mike looked at her and in that moment, she saw pain that she never had seen before. She knew that Mike and Jordan had some sort of bond, but this was different. This was the type of pain that you see in a Nicholas Sparks movie. She didn't know what to say to him, she wanted to say something but nothing she could think of really seemed right.

The days and nights seemed to get longer. When a person only thinks about one thing during the day and then they can't sleep and they think about that one thing, the normal twenty-four hour day seems to have turned into a thirty-six hour day. Even though it was still only the normal twenty-four hour day. Kate found out from her algebra teacher that she was starting to fall asleep in class when her teacher nudged her awake and handed her a tissue for that tiny bit of drool that was coming out of her mouth. Normally all of the other students in the class would chuckle and point. However, they didn't know what Kate was going through by not knowing anything about where Jordan was, or what was happening to her; they knew it was bad and they kept their mouths shut.

Nine

Jordan woke up and there was more food. It seemed like this was becoming a routine. She had no sense of time, she didn't know how long she had been there. She looked around and noticed there were shorts and a sports bra. She thought that seemed odd. It was the kind of outfit that MMA fighters wear. She wasn't an MMA fighter. She had only ever done Tae Kwon Do. So why would this be here? And why? While she pondered these questions, she realized that she was eating and hadn't remembered picking it up. But it still didn't make sense why the outfit. It was white, with black ink blots on it. She stared at the ink blots, and she thought that one of them looked like a boxing glove. She wondered what a shrink would think about that. Sitting on a bed, obviously kidnapped, eating a sandwich, seeing ink blots on the white MMA shorts that had no business being where they were.

She had been there for, well she didn't know how long, but she was there. Food appeared when she slept. She never saw or heard anyone else.

She woke up and looked at the plate, there was a sandwich, roast beef this time with celery and chips with water. She felt the presence before she saw it. He was leaning against the wall wearing jeans, they hung on his hips and you could see the waistband of his underwear; he wasn't skinny, he was built and muscular. He was also wearing a black t-shirt. She felt like someone turned a cold air vent onto her body. She was suddenly cold all over her body and she went rigid. Then he spoke to her, "Hello again Jordan. I am Elijah." When he spoke, she felt not only cold, but like someone had poured ice down her spine. She couldn't move, she was paralyzed with fear. "Now, you have no need to fear." He said. "Let me tell you how things work. Go ahead and eat while I explain." Jordan still could not move, she didn't think that any amount of hunger could have made her take a bite of her food in that moment. "Now here is how things work. This is your room. When you are not training or fighting, you will be here. You will be escorted to training and fights. If you attempt to escape, there will be consequences! Now you aren't speaking, but I can understand that you probably have some questions. You are an excellent fighter, and people are going to compete for you! You should feel honored. I chose you because you are the trifecta! Bold, beautiful, and an amazing fighter! People will pay a lot of money for you! But for now, you and I will get to know each other!" And with that, he stood up and took his shirt off. Every muscle in Jordan started to scream in terror. But she didn't know if there was actually any sound coming out of her mouth.

Ten

Jordan woke up the next morning, or what she assumed was morning. All over her hurt so bad she could barely move. The tears started coming before she realized they were there. That was not how she had envisioned that night. She had always thought it would be with her husband on their wedding night. But not that.

There was a knock on the door a while later, and then a man came in. It wasn't Elijah. It was a tall black man. He came in and handed her some clothes. "Here, there is a shower over there on the wall. Then get dressed and knock on the door."

"Then what?" Jordan asked.

"Then we train." He replied.

"I don't think that I can." She said, her voice cracked in the middle of her sentence.

He looked down at the floor, almost ashamed and reached in his pocket and handed her some blue gel capsules. "I am sorry, these might help." And he left. She looked at them and she was pretty sure that it hadn't mattered what they were, she would have taken them in the hopes that they would take the pain away. But they said Advil on them. She was almost disappointed. She didn't want to take drugs, but she wasn't sure if anything else would take the pain away. The very pit in her soul, something to fill it or take it away.

She got up and she felt every muscle in her whole body ache in pain. She undressed and turned the water on and waited for it to get warm then stepped in. She washed her body slowly, feeling every bruise and pain in her whole body. Tears streamed down her face during the whole shower. She allowed herself that. While drying off, she made a promise that she would never cry except when she was alone. She would not show them her pain. She had a feeling that the "training" would show her weaknesses. But crying was not a weakness, she just preferred to do it alone and not show "them" whoever "them" was that she was in pain. She dressed in the clothes that the black man had given her and she braided her hair. She didn't have a mirror, so she would have to assume that it was ok. She went to the door, took a deep breath, and knocked.

Eleven

The door opened and the black man appeared. He looked her over and nodded for her to step out. "My name is Mason. You can call me Mase. I will be your handler and your trainer. There are too many guards for you to try to escape, so don't even waste time trying to come up with a way. I am going to tell you that everyone who is here has qualifications that supersede your own and you have NO WAY OUT. I am your trainer, so it is my duty to push you hard and help you not get hurt. Do you understand?"

"Yes. What am I training for?" Jordan asked.

They stopped walking and Mase put his hands on his hips. "Look, the less you know for now, the better. It isn't going to help you get through this."

"Do you really think after last night, that anything you tell me could make things worse?"

Mase looked at her, and he had eyes that looked deep into your soul, so when he said it, she believed him. "Yes." And he turned and kept walking. They were in what seemed like a giant warehouse. Boxing rings, weights, speed bags, and punching bags. And everywhere she looked was men with automatic weapons.

He walked over to some weights and said here are some lifting exercises, start with those. "Use light weights, since you are sore." And for a moment, she saw it again, the guilt and shame in his eyes. It was only a flicker. But with the sight of guilt and shame in his eyes, she felt hope!

Two hours later, Mace took her back to her room. "Do some stretches and eat and take a nap.. I will be back later and we will train again." Jordan walked into her room and she felt like she hadn't worked out in years. Whatever muscle didn't hurt before (as if that was even possible) definitely hurt now. She noticed a plate of food on the table again. Lots of vegetables, and some chicken strips and some cottage cheese and some orange juice. She laid on the bed under the covers and before she could start crying she fell asleep.

Jordan didn't know how long she had been sleeping, but she woke up. Pretty sure it was because her stomach was growling. She sat up and grabbed the plate and started eating. She felt like she was trying to put some pieces together. What was this place? What did they want from her? Training? Fights? What for? What was the end game here? Before she knew it, everything was gone. She laid down again and tried to stay warm. She closed her eyes and everything started running through her mind again. She tried to push everything else out and focus on her friends. And Kate, always being able to make her laugh. That day with Mike and how he made her feel. His friendship. The afternoon that she was taken and what happened. Jordan's thoughts drifted to that afternoon. She had been walking out of the locker room and he was there waiting for her. She hadn't thought, and it was like he had read her mind. Their bags hit the ground at the same time and they were in each other's arms in a second. She had never kissed anyone like that. She finally pushed him away, knowing that if she didn't stop this, then she didn't think she could control herself. She fought the fog that was drifting in on her brain. After that is when things got fuzzy. She picked up her bag and left. As she was getting into her car, she felt something behind her and someone grabbed her and that was it. That was all she could remember. This frustrated her, she didn't like not having control.

Twelve

Jordan woke up to a light knock on the door. She got up and went to the door. She knocked and it opened and Mace was there. She stepped out and started walking. "So what are we going to do now?" Jordan asked.

Mace kept walking and laid out the training for her. He told her that they would go to the gym and they would practice and then she would have to fight. "So these fights, are they against other girls that were working out this morning?" Jordan asked.

Mace took a breath and said "you aren't going to let this go are you?"

Jordan glanced at him while walking and said, "I think that if I know what is coming, then I can be prepared."

"I don't know that being more prepared can actually be a thing here. But if that is the way you want it, I will tell you what you want to know." Mace said.

A barely audible "Yes" came from Jordan.

"Ok." He took a deep breath. "You will fight other girls. The guests will place bets on the fight. Then they will place bids on the winner of the fight. The bid winner will get to spend the night with you. Fights take place on the weekends." He looked at the floor when he said it and when he was done, he looked up at her. Jordan took a shuddering breath and closed her eyes. Then she opened her eyes and said "Ok." And she turned to start walking again. Mace must've realized that she was planning to keep it all in. So he walked very slowly to help give her time to process. He didn't need to tell her not to show weaknesses in the gym. They seemed to have a connection, some sort of unspoken understanding. They had the ability to communicate to each other without speaking. "Our strategy in the beginning is to go very slowly, make the other girls think that you have no skills. Then they won't bring out their A game right away. And you will have the advantage. Take them out before they realize what is happening. But after the first couple fights, we will no longer have that advantage. Then we will have to tap into those skills that you have." Mace said. "So while we are in the gym today, don't show your A game.

She nodded. "I am still pretty sore so that won't be a problem."

They got into a ring and she got her gloves on. And Mace got ready with focus targets. They worked out and Jordan played her part well. Missing a lot of punches and falling a lot. She noticed that other girls working out were watching her. Mace was a tough trainer. In the back of her mind, she thought she could actually learn a lot from him. He told her that since she only knew Tae Kwon Do, she was going to have to learn some other things too. This is MMA, that means mixed martial arts. She didn't know how to feel about that. Not that she minded learning from others, she just had always loved Tae Kwon Do so much that she felt like she was almost betraying it by learning something else. The started working on some Brazilian Jui Jit Su. She felt very anxious about this. She wasn't excited about letting anyone into her personal space right now, especially someone that she wasn't punching. So she found herself breathing very hard. At one point Mace had her in a hold where they were basically hugging and although she was controlled, she was almost hyperventilating. He held her and said "I know, but slow your breathing down so you can think of something else."

There was that unspoken communication. He knew what she was thinking about before she even said it. She focused all her attention on clearing her mind and thinking about the one person who could always calm her down. And she slowed her breathing down and she was able to remember the moves he had told her to get out of the hold.

"Good job. That is one hell of a double tap kick you got there! I am impressed. That is enough for today." They started walking back to her room. "You are doing a good job. I know that it is hard. And I can't tell you how to feel, or what to do. But just focus on the training." Mace told her. Jordan looked at him, and for a moment she saw it again. The guilt and shame. She wondered what his story was. How did he end up here? Did he choose to be here? Without saying a word, because she didn't know what to say; she walked into her room and there was a bowl of stew with some bread. She debated on whether to take a shower first or to eat. She settled on the shower, and a good cry. She was so tied up in knots. She didn't know what to do. She missed her dad and her brother and Kate but mostly she missed Mike. She knew that if he hugged her right now, she would always be safe and nothing could ever hurt her again. She finished her shower and put on the clothes laid on the bed for her. She cuddled up in the bed and ate the soup and bread. It was ironically delicious. She had half expected the food to be bland and gross. She finished and cuddled up on the bed. Tears were flowing. She had thought she was done crying, but the tears were just flowing as Mike and Kate's faces flashed in her eyes. The last moments of spending time with them flowed into her mind.

THIRTEEN

In the days following Jordan's disappearance, Mike and Kate had worked out a schedule of being at the house to make sure that they were eating and at least trying to sleep. When Kate got there to take the later part of the evening, her and Mike decided to go for a stroll for a bit and take a walk. "Mike, how are you doing?" Kate asked. They had been closer than Mike had ever thought he would be with Kate. Or closer than he wanted to be with any other woman than Jordan.

"I don't know. Every time I think I am doing ok, I get lost in not knowing what is going on or where she is. Anger and guilt for not staying with her that night." Mike answered.

"You can't blame yourself for what happened. She has come home on her own now for years. Why would that day have been any different?" Kate responded.

"I know, but if I had been with her, it may not have happened." Mike said, holding his head as he walked.

"Maybe, but if it hadn't happened that day, then it probably would have happened the next time you weren't with her." Kate answered.

"Yea maybe." He said. "I just can't get to that understanding."

And with that, they headed back to the house.

Fourteen

Jordan was woken up to a knock at the door again. She loved working out, but this situation was less than ideal. Under different circumstances, she might have enjoyed working out. The facility, the training, the trainer. She got up and went to the door, she wanted to eat before this. The door opened and she saw Mace, "I slept late, I haven't eaten yet."

"Ok, go eat." Mace said. She walked back into the room and Mace followed and leaned against the door. "How do you like the food?"

Jordan shrugged. "I used to make apple slices and then melt some peanut butter and drizzle it over the slices and then melt some Nutella and drizzle it over them and the peanut butter."

"I like apples too. But banana's are my favorite." Mace said. Jordan half smiled.

"So what is your story?" Jordan ventured an ask.

Mace looked down at the floor. "I have a long checkered past. How I ended up here, doesn't matter."

"It just looks like you don't like it sometimes." Jordan said.

"My feelings are not important." Mace said.

Jordan looked down at her now empty plate. "I don't think anyone's feelings here matter."

Mace half nodded and also looked at her plate. Are you ready to go?"

They went to train. Mace seemed to push her harder than he had recently. If she messed up, he yelled at her more than he has in past workouts. This tended to draw a lot of attention. The first time he yelled she was shocked, almost hurt. Everyone stared. She looked at him startled and caught a tiniest of smiles. She then realized what he was doing. He was drawing a lot of attention to her mistakes and if she acted wounded, then the others might not put forth their full effort, thinking that she is an easy target. Hours of this went by. She was extremely frustrated by the time the workout was over. She didn't like doing things wrong, and she had never been yelled at before. She wracked her brain to think of a time while training, even growing up that her dad had ever yelled at her and her brother, but she couldn't. Not even one time. They walked back to her room in silence. "Are the other girls… like me? Prisoners?" Jordan asked when they got to her room.

Mace looked at the floor and then looked her in the eye. "Yes." He said it firmly, but again she heard that faint guilt in his voice. She turned and went into her room. She looked over and saw meatloaf and vegetables with a plate of apples and peanut butter and Nutella drizzled over them. She started to cry seeing them. She longed to be home with her father, and her friends. She missed being at school and working out with Mike and running with Kate. The apple's reminded her of everything that she missed. But she was also happy to see them. It was a small comfort to know that she kind of had a friend here. She sat and ate her apple's first and then the rest of her food. She reminisced about her home and her friends with tears streaming down her face while enjoying her food. Then she took a shower! She laid down under her covers and thought about what was going to happen to her. She remembered the night that she met Elijah and what he had done to her. She hadn't been able to say the words out loud, or even picture the words in her mind. She was having enough trouble keeping the pictures out of her mind. She enjoyed the training, it helped her keep her mind off of it all. But in times like this when she was alone in her room she couldn't keep it out of her mind. She would close her eyes to try and fall asleep fast to not think about it, but that was all she could see. His body, his breath. She cried at the thought of what happened. She then felt something that she hadn't expected. She got mad at Mace. She felt connected to him and that he didn't want to be here or be a part of this. So why was he then? Why didn't he do anything? Why hadn't he saved her, or the other girls? Why did they deserve this? He knew what was going on and he did nothing! She was so angry she wanted to scream. She didn't realize that she was suddenly sitting up! And the tears were angry tears. She was angry with Elijah for what he had done to her, and for what he had taken from her! But she was more angry with Mace for standing by and letting it happen. No, he was allowing it to happen. He had the knowledge and the training to do something about it and he did nothing. He wasn't her friend. He was her enemy just like Elijah. She didn't get much sleep that night, anger fueled her every thought.

FIFTEEN

The next morning she was still mad. Her body was twitching mad. She could barely eat. Then there was a knock on the door. She walked to the door and knocked and it opened. She walked out and stalked past him and kept walking. Mace caught up to her and kept walking too. He didn't talk. Jordan wanted to confront him, but she was never the type of person to get into arguments. She started to lift weights and was pushing harder than usual. Mace didn't have to give her instructions, she knew what to do and she started while Mace walked a bit aways and leaned against the wall. Mace walked over to her after a while and said "Slow down, this isn't a race."

"Why not? I better get as good as I can be. Nobody is going to save me. You are supposed to train me, but in reality you don't care." Jordan spat back at him while doing bicep curls.

"What are you talking about?" Mace said with clear confusion.

"I'm just saying that I am the only one who is going to be able to help myself from not getting..." She stopped and turned to look at him. "You could stop this if you wanted to, but you don't. You just sit there and do what you are told. You don't care about me." At this point, everyone had stopped what they were doing and were staring. Without looking around, Mace stood up and grabbed her arm and started pushing her out of the workout area into the hallway away from everyone else.

"What the hell are you doing?" He asked, pushing her against the wall. "What is wrong with you? Are you trying to get us all killed?"

"You are letting this happen to us! You could stop it! You could call someone and they could find us and instead you are just standing by doing nothing and we have to fight and get, and get raped because you won't stand up for what is right!" She yelled back at him. And that was it, she had finally said the words. And he just stared at her. "He raped me." And the tears started flowing and she couldn't stop them.

Mace looked at her, but she couldn't look at him. Mace put his arm against the wall as another fighter walked past with a guard so they couldn't see Jordan. He leaned close once they had passed and said "Listen to me closely! You have to stay strong! You have to do what you are told. You only put yourself at risk by making a scene. You need to calm down! I know that this is a lot to hold onto and not break but you have to. You hear me? I know you can do this better than any other girl here. You can do this. You can beat them."

"Oh yea, and what about after the fight huh? How am I supposed to stay strong during that?" Jordan said, finally looking at him.

He closed his eyes and shook his head. "Close your eyes and go somewhere else." He stood up straight with his hands on his hips and motioned towards her room. "Your first fight is tomorrow. There will be a lot of people in the training area and only one ring. You can't scream out or ask for help. You will be shot immediately. You have to understand. You have to! It isn't just dangerous for you! It is for all of us, the guards, trainers, and the other girls if you don't listen. Jordan, do you understand?"

They had reached her room and he had stopped and so did she. She was looking at the ground. "Jordan?"

"Yes, I understand." She said it very quietly and never looked at him. She walked into the room and closed the door behind her. She didn't want to see him anymore. She laid down on the bed without taking a shower or anything and she just cried.

Sixteen

She woke up the next morning or what she thought was morning and there was a knock on the door. She didn't get up. She wondered maybe she could 'call in sick'. What if she refused to get up. She didn't even know what time it was. She didn't want to do anything. This time the person knocking didn't wait for a response. Mace walked in and laid something on the end of her bed and sat on the chair. She didn't say anything. She just looked at him. They sat silently for a few minutes. Mace finally looked at her and said "The fight is tonight. You can win. But you are going to have stuff your feelings way down deep. Don't look at anything except the other fighter. Feel the ring and know it. Don't look outside of it. It is going to hurt, and it is going to be the hardest thing you have ever done. Your opponent is a good fighter, and she is bigger, but she isn't as fast as you are. But you can win and you have to fight hard. Get some rest today. You will be brought food, do some stretching and I will see you this evening. Do you have any questions?" She did nothing. "Do you need anything?" He waited a moment while looking at her and then looked at the floor and then got up and left.

She didn't know what to think. She was still mad at him. But she thought that she was going to need to find a way past that in order to make it through tonight. But she didn't want to think about anything right now. So, she closed her eyes and thought about Mike. The last time they were together. She ran through the whole afternoon. Every single punch and kick. And then the conversation and the kiss. She let her mind wander to that afternoon with Mike. It was something she often dreamed of. Being romanced by him. His hands running through her hair. He hugged her and kissed her neck. She suddenly didn't want to have this dream anymore either. She shifted her thoughts to Kate. Running with Kate had always been fun. She turned to one of those runs where they were joking and laughing and having fun. She let herself drift off with those thoughts.

Seventeen

She woke up and felt oddly rested. She decided to take a shower and then eat the food left for her. After her shower she braided her hair and then looked at the pile that Mace had left on her bed. There were MMA shorts and a sports bra. They were like a camo style but a black camo she had never seen before. She thought that the style was sleek and gave her the sense of power; like a multi-millionaire in a black suit could make everyone board meeting quiver. She put it on and felt indestructible. She ate and then waited. She was done eating for a while and had been doing some punching combinations with a boxer's bounce in her room. The longer she waited the more anxious she got. She had never been in a fight before. She had trained and spared but never had an actual fight. She was pacing her room and then there was a knock. She stopped in her tracks. Mace came in, "You look good."

Jordan didn't know what to say to that. She thought that Thanks might be the wrong word in this situation. So, she just stood there. He had tape in his hands and gloves. He taped her wrists up and put the gloves on. They were white on the knuckles and black on the sides. "Are you ready for this?" Mace asked.

"Is anyone ever ready for this?" Jordan asked, as they were walking. "So what happens?"

Mace never took his eyes off her. "When we go to the ring..." but Jordan interrupted.

"I know about that part. I mean after." Jordan said with her arms crossed across her chest.

"Well after the fight, the spectators will essentially pay for the winner in an auction. When the winner of the auction is chosen, they are brought back to the room." Mace said, this is the part where he refused to look at her.

"And then what?" She asked when he hesitated. "I need it all Mace."

He shook his head and you could tell that he didn't want to say the rest. "And then, the winner does what they want. Nothing is off limits." And a tear streamed down his face and he wiped it before she could notice.

It was at that moment that Jordan had looked up, and she saw the tear. "What happened to you?"

The tears were free flowing and he couldn't stop them. "I was an amazing fighter, with a really big chip on my shoulder. I knew I was next to win the title. It wouldn't be long before I had my shot and nobody could stop me. I had a great girlfriend who was pregnant. I had a huge gambling problem. She would have been smart to leave then for her sake and the baby's! She could have saved them both! I was in debt that I could never get out of. I made a deal that would get me out of debt. If I won he would wipe out all my debt. If I lost I had to become his trainer. I was so cocky that I wasn't even training. When the baby came, I was overjoyed and she told me that she was going to leave. And I swore to her that I would never gamble again, and convinced her to stay. The night of the title fight came. And I jumped in without even a thought that I could be distracted and loose. What I didn't know was that he had kidnapped my wife. Before the fight even started, he got my attention from the box. He was holding my baby boy and my wife was there. I could see the fear on her face! I tried to get to her but they wouldn't let me out. He put a gun up to her head and shot her." There was a long pause. Then he continued. "He had bet against me to make money, and he had killed her to ensure that I was distracted enough to lose. And he had my son. He still has my son."

Silent tears fell from Jordan's eyes. She couldn't imagine. "It was Elijah wasn't it." It wasn't really a question because she knew the answer. Mace nodded. But she didn't need confirmation. "Do you know where your son is?"

"No, he gives me pictures but that is it. I don't know if I will ever find him." Mace said.

"What is his name?" Jordan asked.

"She named him Samuel. He would be two now." Mace was barely able to get it out. "I have never told anyone this."

"Isn't there a way to find him?" She suddenly felt a mission to her and an obligation to Mace to help find his son. He was a hostage just like her. And they needed to work together to get their freedom.

"I don't know." Mace said, shaking his head. "But now we need to focus on tonight. We need to get through this."

"I would rather focus on something else." Jordan said.

"Ok here is how it's going to go. We go out there and you will get into the ring. Remember what I said, don't look around. Look at your opponent and that is it. Focus on what is about to happen. Focus on her and anticipate the next move to be made. Your job is to get through this." Mace said. "Are you ready?"

Jordan nodded. Suddenly she felt faint, and she thought she was having trouble breathing. Mace noticed at once. He steered her towards a wall and gave her a paper bag to breathe into. It was like he had anticipated that she would have a panic attack before walking through there. A few minutes went by and she calmed down. Mace stood up and waited. Without saying it, his body told her "Whenever you're ready." After another minute, she got up and left the bag on the bed and when she looked up at him, it was like a switch had been turned and she was a different person. They walked in silence to the training room. When they got to the door, she could hear cheering and people before he even opened the door. He opened the door and she saw the ring and she didn't look at anything else. She could hear the people cheering and her brain started to panic. She quieted it by going through forms in her mind. She walked up to the ring and looked at Mace. He said "Stay focused on what skills you have and anticipate her moves." And with that Jordan stepped into the ring.

Eighteen

The ring was big. She had only seen something like this in MMA fights on HBO. She didn't let her emotions show on her face at all. She stuffed them all down like Mace told her to. She focused on her opponent. She was about four inches taller than Jordan was and had red hair. Jordan had started in her bounce when she climbed into the ring. Jordan looked at her. She wondered what her name was or what her story was and how she ended up here. She didn't think that she was from her town. She would have known if there was a girl her age missing. She wiped those thoughts from her mind. She didn't want to feel bad for this girl. She did feel bad for her, but she didn't want to think that they were the same because then she didn't think that she would be able to fight her. She didn't want to win, knowing what would happen after, but Mace had told her the losing is way worse than winning. She was scared to think of what that meant. So, she wanted to win. That wasn't true either, she didn't want to be there at all. But for lack of better choices winning was the best of the worst options. She was also scared to win, because if she won, what would happen to the other girl? What other choice did she have? Unfortunately, here, she had to choose the best of the worst option. She knew the other girl was doing the same. She looked at Mace, she wasn't sure what to do next. Like was there going to be a bell or something. He held his hand up and motioned for her to wait and stay there. Just then, she heard a speaker system turn on. Then she heard a voice that was like ice cold water running down her back again. Elijah's voice boomed through the sound system. "Ladies and Gentlemen! Welcome to another night of Double Beat Down!! Our opponents today are… In the White corner, we have The Ginger!! And in the Black corner we have a New fighter!! Double Tap!! You have seen the fighters… Place your bets!!" Elijah waited and watched an iPad that he was holding. After about a minute, he said into the mic "20 seconds!" When he said this, Jordan noticed that the other fighter had sped up her bounce. She followed suit. She started to take some quick breaths to calm her mind. But eyes on the opponent. She could feel all of the emotions welling up inside her body ready to betray her and spill out through her eyes! She shoved them down and shook her head to wipe them away. She needed to feel anger to get through this, she didn't know if anything other than that would work. Begrudgingly, she looked at Elijah and remembered that night. Her instinct was to wipe the thoughts away. But she kept them in the forefront of her mind. She remembered his breath. The weight of his body on top of hers. There it was. She felt the swell of anger rise up inside of her like a tidal wave. She looked at her opponent and knew that this was the only way. Elijah's voice rang out "Fighters!! Fight!"

Jordan didn't have time to contemplate the nickname she had been given because The Ginger came out swinging! Jordan was ready for it by the time she got there. Jordan sidestepped and kneed her in the stomach as hard as she could. But Ginger recovered before Jordan had time to land another strike. And swung at her again with a vicious hook. Jordan blocked but was still in the mind frame of being defensive and even though she knew that the fight was going to happen and was literally in the middle of it, she couldn't believe that this girl was actually trying to hurt her. She missed the opening to punch the ginger in the face and was rewarded with a vicious jab to her nose. She felt it break and blood spilled everywhere. She stumbled backwards but recovered quickly and she lunged at the Ginger with a flying punch in the face. Now they both had a broken nose. Jordan didn't miss anything twice, she continued to punch and the Ginger did too. She got one into the ribs that made her stumble back. The Ginger jumped up and started punching Jordan in the face. This part seemed surreal to Jordan, she could see the punches coming but all she felt was a puff of air. She thought she should feel more than that. She assumed that the Ginger wasn't missing her face. But she felt nothing.

She threw a hook as hard as she could and landed it right on her jaw. And the Ginger hit her knees. Jordan kicked her in the stomach. Jordan thought that would be the end of the round or something so she just stood there for a second, which was a second too long. The Ginger flung her leg out and swept Jordan off her feet. She was on top of her in a second and started punching her face again.

But again, she couldn't feel it. But this time she had either been knocked dazed or knocked out because now she was seeing things. There was a man between her and the Ginger and he was taking all of the punches for her. She couldn't really describe him but he was amazingly beautiful and he didn't flinch at any punch, and he never punched back. For a moment, she was dazzled by his brilliance. Then she seized the moment and wrapped her feet around her neck and gave her strongest punch. She felt The Ginger go limp and she let go of her legs, she crumpled on the floor.

They both lay there for what felt like an eternity. Then she rolled over and pulled her knee's up under her and got to her feet. She looked around and realized there was blood everywhere. She assumed that most of it was from her. She looked over at her opponent and prayed that she wasn't dead. She just stared at her. She kept telling her legs to move and see but nothing happened. There was so much blood. What if she had killed her? Could she have killed her?

"And the winner is... Double Tap!" Elijah's voice rang out and jolted her back to reality. She didn't know what to do. In a moment, Mace was at her side.

Nineteen

"Listen to me." He spoke with urgency. "In a moment, the doctor will take you and patch you up. Then you will be taken to a room. Don't fight it, it will only make it worse. You can get through this."

"Did I kill her?" Was all she could manage to get out.

Mace looked at the other girl and the couple of people standing around her. "No, she just knocked out, probably with a broken jaw."

At that moment, an older man walked over to her, and he had little spectacle glasses on. There was something about him that just made her want to hug him and cry on his shoulder. She looked at Mace and he nodded at her to go with him. She looked at the other girl and two others carried her off in the direction the doctor was heading.

She hadn't realized it but this whole time Elijah had been talking. But she had no idea about what. She followed the doctor. They went into a locker type room. "Sit down there," the doctor told her. She sat on a table like you see for boxers in the movies. Without comment, she sat down. It was only then that she felt every single blow that The Ginger had thrown and landed on her body. A little squeak came out when her butt hit the bench. The doctor turned and peered at her over his spectacles. "You took one hell of a beating out there tonight. I am actually surprised that you are even sitting here right now." He was now standing right in front of her. She wondered why he wore the glasses if he never looked through them. "She really laid into you, and it looked like you didn't even notice. How is that possible?" He wondered.

She didn't know if she should say anything about the man to this old man or if he would hand her a straight jacket. But really, who was he going to tell that would give two hoots if she was seeing people? But she decided against it, and said nothing. "Ok, let's fix you up." He stitched a cut above her eye and put some stuff on her lip that made it stop bleeding. And then he looked at her and said something that she didn't expect. "That is about all I can do for you, except this." He held up a needle.

"What is that?" Jordan asked, she was about ready to jump off the table. She didn't do drugs, she never had. Some people she knew had done stuff, but she had never had the desire. She didn't have the desire to start now either.

"This is some medication pain. Along with taking away your pain, it might make your brain a bit…" he hesitated and then continued, "well, foggy the next few hours."

The look on his face was compassion. She felt that he was actually trying to help her. Like he wanted her to not have to feel the events that would soon take place. To spare her heart the breaking of what would transpire in the next few hours. Although she felt that no matter the amount of drugs he gave her wouldn't fog her brain to forget what was going to happen. "No thanks," She said.

"Jordan, not taking it is noble. But you don't have to do things this way." He said to her while trying to put a comforting hand on her shoulder.

"Clearly you know what is going on here. Why don't you stop it and save everyone?" Jordan stated looking up to stare him straight in the eye.

He didn't falter in their stare off. "I wish I could help you more." He nodded at one of the guards. He walked over and took her by the arm and led her out.

The guard walked her down some hallways she had never been down. She wondered how big the building was. With every step, she felt pain shooting through her body. Maybe it was pain, or maybe it was fear about what happened to the other girl, and what was about to happen to her. They stopped at a door and the guard opened it. He nodded at her to go in. She took a moment and took a deep breath and straightened her shoulders and walked in.

It was a very upscale and lavishly decorated room. She saw a huge bed. And elaborately decorated bed sheets and comforter. Next to the bed was a red chair, and in it sat a man smoking a cigar and he had a little glass of some brownish liquid in it. When she took another step into the room. She recognized who was in the chair. Elijah. She gasped and tried to run out of the room, before she knew it he was behind her and he grabbed her hair and threw her on the bed. She tried to scramble away but he grabbed her foot and yanked her back towards him. When he slapped her in the face. She was dazed and seemed to lose consciousness.

Twenty

Jordan woke up the next morning and tried to sit up in bed. She winced and squeaked with pain. She felt the movement before she saw him. She grabbed the covers and yanked them up her naked body. He was buckling his belt and he looked at her and said "Get up and get dressed, the guard outside will take you to your room. You have two weeks to rest before your next fight."

She said nothing and he turned and walked out. She had never encountered someone so cold hearted. She waited a few minutes before getting up. She finally got up and got out of bed with tears streaming down her face. She felt every single movement of every muscle. When she stood up she got dressed and wanted to get out of there as soon as possible. She went to the door and knocked. A guard opened the door and took her back to her room. When she got there she walked in and as soon as she heard the door shut, she went straight to her shower and turned on the water. She didn't know if there was more coming from the shower head or from her eyes. She felt so disgusting. Between the fight and the second fight she didn't think that any amount of soap and water would get her clean. She scrubbed and scrubbed until her skin was red. She cried and cried. She finally turned off the water. She couldn't bear to look at herself. She put on some shorts and a shirt and she got into bed. She tried to close her eyes and fall asleep, but visions of the night before kept seeping their way into her mind. She kept seeing the whole night replay in her mind and she couldn't stop it and she certainly didn't want to think about the second fight. So she let her mind drift to the first one. Then she remembered when that man was in front of her taking every blow for her. There was no explanation for it. But she focused on his face, for some reason focusing on his face gave her peace and she was finally able to fall asleep.

Twenty-one

In the morning, Jordan woke up to a tray of food sitting next to her. She tried to move and her whole body screamed in pain. She could barely reach forward and grab a grape. When she did finally move forward, she realized there was some Advil sitting next to her glass of water. She knew if she moved her body, she would be less sore sooner. But she just couldn't bring her body to move. It was odd, but she felt like normally Mace would have been there by then to bring her to the training room. She decided that she was going to stay in bed until he came to get her.

Mace never came. Food was delivered at lunch time and again at dinner. Someone brought it into her room. She pretended to be sleeping each time. She didn't want to get stuck in a conversation with anyone.

Sometime around mid day the dr came in to check her out. He gently nudged her and asked her to wake up. She wasn't really sleeping, so she just rolled over and looked at him. "How are you feeling?" He asked her. She shrugged. He pursed his lips together and nodded, "Can you sit up for me?" He held his hand out to help her sit up, and she moved, trying not to show him how much pain she was in, and she sat up on the bed with her legs over the side. She was wearing a pair of loose cotton shorts and a loose tank top. He first looked at the cuts on her face and changed the butterfly bandages on her cut above her eye. He felt around her face looking for broken bones. Her cheekbone was massively swollen. "I am sure that hurts but I don't think anything is broken in there." He lifted her shirt and looked at her back, he gently felt around, knowing how much pain it caused her. He gently helped her back into bed, and lifted her shirt in the front, but kept her carefully covered. He felt on her ribs very gently, but even as gentle as he was being, it caused her to wince and pull away in that one spot. "Well that rib is most likely cracked I am sorry to say. Take these." He said, handing her some tablets. She didn't want to, but she took it anyway. "It is oxycodone, it will help with the pain. So I am surprised to see the small amount of injuries that you actually have. I thought that I would see more severe injuries than you have."

He said it as though he was trying to pry something out of her. It was almost like he knew that there had been someone else in the ring protecting her from injury, but was waiting for her to tell him about it. She opted not to, and instead focused on the other thing he was saying.

"I'm afraid that is basically what I can do for you. You need to rest. You will have a few days to rest," he looked her in the eye, "no one will bother you!" His eyes reassured her that she wouldn't have to train and she would have no other unexpected guests. She closed her eyes and tears fell. It was the smallest of reassurances, but he wiped a tear from her eye. And with that he got up and left. She kept her eyes closed and let the tears fall until she fell asleep.

Twenty-two

Days came and went, Jordan didn't know how many. Everyday she got up and showered and moved around a bit and tried to stretch out. The doctor came occasionally to check on her. Each time he made reference to her minor injuries and probed why she thought she had so few, based on the beating she took, but she usually just shrugged him off and didn't answer. She sometimes opened her mouth like she was going to tell him, but then stopped herself. She felt connected to him, almost like you would a grandfather. But then she thought she better not say anything because he would think that she was crazy.

She tried to stretch out and ease the soreness and pain but it seemed to work and then after she woke up again, she felt worse than she did before. The tears seemed as uncontrollable as the soreness. They came with as much vengeance as the pain. Her heart cried out with each tear from the pain she felt so deep within her soul. She got angry every time it happened. She hated crying but she couldn't stop it either. She finally gave in and just let it happen when it did. With each tear she felt the pain of everything that had happened to her so far. Being taken from her family and friends, the rapes, the beating, the fight. She let the tears go hoping that it would help her soul find healing in them.

Twenty-three

She didn't know how many days had gone by but food had been delivered three times a day. In the evenings, there were two tablets with her supper. She took them so that it eased the pain and it helped her get around. But last night she only took one. She was pretty sure that the name the doctor had mentioned was probably addictive. And she wanted nothing to do with that. She decided that if she needed it in the morning, she would take it, but not before.

In the morning, there was a knock on the door. Mace walked in. She was sitting in bed, but she had already showered and stretched, and for the most part she felt pretty good. She hadn't needed the other pill that morning. "How are you feeling?" He asked but never looked her in the eyes.

She was looking at him. Some sort of peace had come over her as she had cried all of those tears. "I'm ok."

He nodded, "Do you feel like doing some light training today?"

"Actually, no. I want to do some yoga and stretching and that's it." She told him.

That was the first time he looked at her. "Um well I don't know any yoga."

She stood up and said, "Well I guess that you will be learning from me today then."

He seemed a bit off today and he kind of tripped walking out the door. He usually walked with so much confidence and grace. She wasn't sure if it was the yoga that had him uptight. But it seemed like more than that. It was almost like he was ready to jump out of his skin, she couldn't really place why, or maybe she had no idea what it was that was making him so jumpy. "Jordan, your next fight is tomorrow, it might be different than the last time. If something happens, you need to lay down and cover your head." He looked at her and again he looked jumpy, "do you understand?" This time he almost seemed alarmed that she did understand. He grabbed her arm, "Jordan, I mean it, this is serious!"

"What's wrong? What's gonna happen? What could happen here?" Jordan was starting to feel jumpy too. "Mace come on what is going on?"

"Look, we go into there and do some yoga or whatever, and act normal. Do not bring it up again! Do you understand?" Mace told her again, acting frustrated and jumpy and looking down the hallway.

"Ok." She responded somewhat taken aback. She continued walking into the training area.

She did some yoga and he watched her and the other trainees. She did not see the girl that she fought who knows how long ago now. She prayed a little prayer in her head that the girl was ok. She hadn't ever prayed before, and she wasn't religious but she felt that there was a God. And she was guessing that even though she had been through the world, he was on her side.

Twenty-four

After Lunch the next day, her fighting outfit was delivered. She showered and standing there under the water, she thought about the last time. She remembered every punch she took, and every punch that she delivered. With each thought she remembered, she felt sick to her stomach. She remembered after the fight, and the thought of it made her vomit in the shower drain. She managed to pull herself back together and finish showering. She braided her hair and got dressed in the outfit.

There was a knock on the door and it opened. There was a trainer there. She had seen him in the training area but she didn't know him. "Mace said he will meet you there, and asked me to bring you up," he said.

She stared at him for a second and then walked forwards. "You were the other girls' trainer. The red head. What happened to her?" Jordan asked with some fear of what the answer would be.

Helooked at her and then walked out of the room and was quiet for the rest of the walk. They got to the ring. Then he stopped and stared at her, she felt uncomfortable. He took a deep breath, looked her in the eye and he very quietly said to her, so quiet it was almost inaudible, "If anything happens in there that is out of your control, get down."

"What does that mean?" she asked, feeling uneasy. But he closed the door to the ring and walked away.

It wasn't seconds after the door was closed that she felt a huge punch into her side. Apparently her opponent had not waited for introductions and jumped the second that the doors were closed. She fell to her knees, her face wrenched in pain. She felt a blow to the side of her head, her ears were ringing. She was on the ground. She heard some loud bangs that she couldn't place, she didn't think it was from the blow to her head but she didn't know what it was either. It seemed as though her opponent was also on the ground but she had no idea why because along with the ringing and banging in her ears she was seeing double. But it also seemed like people were running all around instead of watching the fight. But it also seemed like there was no fight either because they were both on the ground.

Then she heard something in her head, again barely audible; "If anything happens in there that is out of your control, get down." It seemed like some of the brain fog she felt was lifting. So she listened to the voice in her head and she stayed down with her hands above her head. It felt like forever but finally she felt someone touch her on the arm. "Jordan! Jordan! It's ok! I am a police officer. You are safe now."

Before she realized it, he had turned her over and was holding her. She could see him and she could see the "SWAT" on his vest and she touched his arms to see that he was real and not a dream. He was real. She took a big breath in and before she could stop it, the tears started rolling down her face. He pulled her close to him and continued to tell her she was safe.

Twenty-five

They walked into the hospital and the receptionist told them where to wait. It was over an hour when the doctor came out and explained that Jordan was being taken for a CT scan. And she had some injuries but nothing life threatening. They were still waiting on some lab work, but so far it looked like there were some injuries that were healing and they were still assessing. However, the scan and labs would give them a better idea of any other problems that might be going on.

Mike finally spoke, "Is she able to talk? Did she say what happened to her? Or who took her?"

The doctor breathed deeply, and said, "She has spoken and she seems fairly lucid. However, events and trauma that she has been through that she said to me are privileged. And what she tells the police is up to her. She has been through quite an ordeal and I encourage you to have patience with her and not to push her to give details about what happened. She will tell you in her own time, whenever that is."

"When can we see her?" Brad asked.

"Well we are waiting to get the results and then a psychologist will be up to talk to her and then we will see. Now if you will excuse me." The doctor gave Brad a reassuring pat on the shoulder and walked away.

Brad sat down and put his head between his hands and started to cry. Josh, who hadn't said a word since the cop walked into the house; sat down beside his dad and put his head and his hand on his father's shoulder and cried. Mike sat next to them not moving or saying anything.

Kate sat two chairs away and silent tears streamed down her face as she imagined all the horrors that her best and closest friend in the world could have gone through. She had always had friends growing up, but never someone who she had felt as close to as Jordan. And someone she actually liked. The tears fell silently for Jordan as she mourned her friend.

Hours went by. They walked and paced and got coffee and waited and waited some more. The doctor walked out the doors into the waiting room and walked up to them. They all stood there not saying a word; just waited as though someone had pressed pause. "My name is Dr. James, we are going to keep her for a while for observation for a few days. But she is asking to see you all." Brad and Josh jumped up and the doctor raised his hand to stop them all and they all stopped in their tracks. "She has a request. She asks that if you are going to cry or ask about what happened, that you not come in. She doesn't want to talk about it and she doesn't want to ask about it. She does want you to know that she believes she is fine and just needs some time."

Brad, Josh, and Kate were ready to go. Kate looked at Mike and he looked at her and said, "I don't think I can do it. I don't think that I can see her like this."

Kate grabbed his hand. "We do this together. We do this for her. She needs us to be strong right now. You can't do this, and I can't do this. But together we can do this." She grabbed his hand, and she looked at Brad and Josh who were also staring at her, and she held out her hand and Brad reached out and took it and held his hand out to Josh. Together, they walked to see Jordan.

She smiled when she saw them. They all hesitantly walked up to her. Kate was the first to step forward and give her a hug. She held her hands out as though she was first asking for permission to hug her and Jordan nodded. Kate never wanted to let her go. Jordan could see that Mike was holding back tears and she reached for his hand. And then her father joined in on the hug and then Mike did too. She never wanted to let them go.

TWENTY-SIX

As Jordan lay in her hospital bed, she contemplated how to ever be herself again. She felt like an alien in someone else's skin. Every movement that used to be so graceful, now felt backwards and awkward. Knowing that she could never go back to who she used to be and that little girl had been robbed from her, how is she supposed to step forward? Her thoughts were interrupted by the nurse who came in to check on her. She was an older African American woman, named Evelyn. Jordan thought she was sweet, in the kind of the way you would expect a mom to be.

"Hey, I didn't interrupt your thoughts, did I?" She asked.

"None that didn't need to be interrupted!" Jordan replied.

Evelyn looked at her carefully. "You know, even though we may not like some thoughts, you still have to have them. It is all part of the process."

"What process?" Jordan asked.

"Getting better." Evelyn replied while putting down the blood pressure cuff.

"I thought the doctor said that I was fine, other than the obvious bruises…." Jordan said with a hint of unease.

"Physically, yes dear! But you also have to get better mentally. And that takes time and a lot of thought. And some of those thoughts aren't always fun or pleasant, and it doesn't happen overnight or after a good night's rest. You need to take time!"

"I'm fine." Jordan replied, straightening her jaw.

"Girl, you can't fool me. I know what you went through, and it isn't going to go away overnight. And ignoring it isn't going to make it go away either. Only one person can help you truly heal after what you went through."

"Yea, I heard the doctor was sending in a shrink." Jordan replied while rolling her eyes.

Evelyn gave a humph to that comment and grabbed her stuff, "That isn't who I was referring to!"

Jordan watched her stalk out of the room. Well if she wasn't talking about the shrink, who was she talking about? Jordan was confused. Evelyn seemed like a lady you didn't want to cross and also that she sometimes already expected you to know the answer to what she was talking about. But how was she supposed to know this? She had just got here, she didn't know everyone in the hospital. And how should she ask about it the next time? Did she even want to ask about it? She really just wanted to forget that the whole thing ever happened! But the more she thought she wanted to forget it, the more she wondered who Evelyn had been referring to.

Sleep wasn't coming easy for Jordan that night. When she closed her eye's, her mind replayed what had happened; which was making her job of forgetting what had happened incredibly difficult. She had fallen asleep but had woken up in a dripping sweat, she thought she was going to scream. When she opened her eye's. Evelyn was next to her with a washcloth wiping her face and shushing her and telling her she was ok. Before she could stop herself, she was in Evelyn's arms crying. Somehow she knew that Evelyn understood, and she didn't have to explain anything to her. "It's ok baby girl! I got you! Can't no one hurt you no more! You go ahead and cry all you need. Get all that bad right out!" Evelyn held her and talked to her while Jordan cried more than she ever had. She cried for all the things that she remembered had happened. She cried for all the things that she didn't remember had happened. She cried for all of the things that she thought she may never forget happened. And yet she was oddly comforted by the fact that she was fairly certain that Evelyn knew each and every one of those reasons. But she didn't know how.

After hours of crying, she must've fallen asleep in Evelyn's arms, she woke up. Evelyn was awake and looked like she hadn't moved a muscle the whole time. Still holding her in the exact same position. Jordan opened her eyes and started to get up, Evelyn helped her adjust to her new position. "I'm sorry about that, I don't know what came over me. I have never done that before in my life, and I am sure you have better things to do."

"Well you were far overdue for a good cry then. It helps to cry, you have deal with all that emotion. Even when you don't even think that you have a reason to. Sometimes I just turn on a good old tearjerker movie and get it all out. It's our way of dealing with things. Nothing to be ashamed of. And no, as a matter of fact, I have nothing better to do, my shift was over hours ago." Evelyn said with a comforting smile.

"Well we don't do that in our house. It's all muscle and punches unless you're bleeding. And I don't think I have ever seen any tearjerker movies." Jordan said.

"Ain't that a shame! You are missing some of the best movies in the world! My Girl, Steel Magnolias, The Notebook, The Pursuit of Happiness, just to name a few; are some of the most emotional movies of all time! They help us move through some of our own emotions sitting on the surface of our own souls and help us move forward."

"If your shift was over, why didn't you go home?" Jordan asked curiously.

"My boy and my husband went home to the good Lord years ago. He has now given me you to look after, so here I am, unless you want me to leave." She said, raising her eyebrow. Jordan shook her head no. "Well alright then, I will sit here and read until you need something. Unless you want to talk."

"Talk about what?" Jordan asked.

"Whatever you want to. School, running, home, what happened, what didn't happen. The color of the tiles... you name it, I can carry on a conversation about it!" Evelyn stated matter a factly.

"I don't want to talk about it. I just want to forget it ever happened." Jordan said flatly.

"Well dear, that is just never going to happen, no matter how hard you try. You need to open up your heart to God and let him in and admit what happened and let him heal you physically and emotionally. Let him into your heart so that he can heal you!" Evelyn said with all her heart.

Jordan stared at her blankly. She didn't know what those words meant, much less what to do with them. And even if she thought that "God" who ever he was, could HEAL her, she couldn't bear the thought of admitting what had happened. She could barely bring herself to think about it, being able to say yes to the rape kit in the Emergency room had actually made her vomit. They had all known she needed it. But they told her that she had to verbally consent. Then she puked. Jordan must've been an open book at that moment because Evelyn read right through her.

"I know that you are struggling with even admitting to yourself what you have been through. But you can't keep ignoring it. You have to march right up to it and punch it square on the nose if that is the phrase you want to use." This earned a smirk from Jordan. She had long since passed doing something as simple as a punch on the nose! "Young lady, you may not be religious, and you may not know who our Lord and savior is. But you will soon learn that you have been saved by him, and all of your wounds can be healed. He can heal your broken heart and make it whole again."

"I don't know, sounds pretty fishy. How do you know that someone didn't just make up all those stories about Jesus?" Jordan questioned.

As though she had answered all of these questions a thousand times before, she took a deep breath, "Honey, we have to have faith. We don't have all of the answers to all of your questions about God and how and why all of these things have happened. But we do know that Jesus did come, he did die for our sins, and he did rise from the dead 3 days later. He is all powerful and he can do anything. And for now, that is all you need to worry about. The rest will come in time. But you have to choose to have faith."

Twenty-seven

In the morning when Jordan woke, Evelyn wasn't there. She had scrambled eggs with bacon and some toast on a tray waiting for her. She had started eating when a woman in a dress suit walked in. "Hello Jordan, I am Dr. Wright, I am a psychiatrist here at the hospital."

Jordan looked at her expectantly, she wasn't really sure what to say.

"So I will be seeing you while you are here, and then doing some follow-ups when you leave."

"Ok. I don't really know what to say." Jordan said.

"Well, we can start by talking about what happened." Dr. Wright said taking out his notebook.

"No." Jordan said. "I don't want to talk about it. I want to leave and never think about it again."

"Ok, why don't you tell me about you. Who you are?"

"It doesn't matter, I am not that person anymore, and I never will be again." Jordan stated.

"Why do you think that you can't be her anymore?" Dr. Wright asked.

"It's all there in the chart right. I am no longer that girl. I can never be her again. So I want to go home and find a new life for myself and start over." Jordan said looking dazily forward as though she could see the future and this new life.

"If you could pick a new life for yourself, what would you pick?" Dr. Wright asked.

"I don't know. I haven't even finished high school yet. I am only sixteen. I don't want to talk about this anymore." Jordan said.

"Ok. Well Jordan, there are some things that I want to talk to you about. If you don't want to talk, then you don't have to, you can just listen. So we know that you were missing for about four weeks. You haven't given us a first time that you were abused. We do know that it happened continuously over that time period, both physically and sexually. So that brings us to the possibility of pregnancy." She carefully watched Jordan for any sign of reaction. She saw nothing. "We will test you for all sexually transmitted diseases and pregnancy. But we need to prepare you for that possibility and discuss your options."

"My options?" Jordan asked

"Well if you are pregnant, we can discuss termination." Dr. Wright stated.

Jordan had never really given it much thought before, but that thought made her stomach turn. Dr. Wright noticed and was lucky to grab the barf bag in time to not get any on her suit. It seemed as though, even being a Doctor, puke wasn't something she was used to dealing with. Luckily, Evelyn walked in at that moment and took charge of the situation. "Well Jordan, I will stop back and talk with you again later." Smoothing her suit as though she was dusting off Evelyn's lack of respect for her.

With a tear-streaked face, Jordan sputtered looking at Evelyn "I do not want to talk anymore, I just want to forget!"

Evelyn took her usual place and began to bustle about taking care of her patient! She was shushing Jordan and telling her not to worry about anything. She didn't have to talk about whatever she didn't want to. And Jordan began to calm down. Jordan told Evelyn that she just wanted to forget everything and go to sleep, and with that she drifted off. The problem with forgetting is that every time she closed her eyes, she replayed the last weeks of her life. And when she didn't have her eyes closed, she could smell him and hear him. When those two things didn't make her skin crawl, she could feel his body on top of her body and she was trying to fight back but she was groggy and felt drunk. And there was something wrong with her hands and feet. Not just that each limb felt like it was one hundred pounds, but she could only move so far before they stopped. Her wrists and ankles were always cold, but only in a little spot. She didn't understand and now matter how much she tried to clear her head, it just wouldn't, it was like a fog that didn't lift. And all she heard was his voice, "Sshhhh, don't speak, and don't try anything. You are mine now." She woke up in a cold sweat again. Jordan realized that Evelyn was over her again.

"It is going to be awfully hard to forget him when you see him every time you close your eyes. But in time, it will come." Evelyn said while looking at her as though she could see right through her.

Jordan stared back at her. "How is it that you always seem to know what is going on inside my head?"

Evelyn handed Jordan her lunch plate and then sat down in the chair. "Well my dear, you see I have been around quite a long time. And I have seen a great many things. And not all of them have been good. So I may have a level of understanding that some people don't. And over my years my dear, I can say that I have forgotten none of those bad things, even the ones I wanted to forget, I still remember."

"So how do you go through every day remembering?" Jordan asked.

"Well, I have been given peace and I am able to move forward through my life knowing that there is a day where I will be in heaven with God, and he is able to help me work through the process." Evelyn said with compassion and understanding.

Jordan closed her eyes. Somehow knowing what she was thinking, Evelyn said, "With Jesus, there will come a day when you close your eyes and that picture that you see now isn't so close to you. And with peace, he has given me a calling. A calling upon my life to help people. Just like he will for you one day. It may not be the same calling, but he has a plan for your life. He has a plan for you!"

"How can you be so sure? God doesn't want me, I am no good to him." Big tears streamed down her face now. "He raped me. He took everything from me. My childhood, my friends, and my innocence."

Evelyn came to her and with the gentlest of touches, she wiped her tears away. "Oh honey! I know that it hurts! And in time, healing will come! But admitting it is part of that process. The other part is going that path with Jesus."

"My family isn't religious. I don't know how to do that." Jordan sighed.

"Oh my dear sweet girl! None of that matters. It doesn't matter if you were raised in a church or have had Jesus in your heart forever or are 80 years old and are just starting out with him." Jordan smiled at her meekly.

Twenty-eight

Jordan had so much swimming around in her head the next morning when Dr. Wright came in the next morning. "Good morning Jordan!" And how are you feeling today?"

"I'm ok." Jordan said, preoccupied.

Dr. Wright looked at Jordan and said "What's the matter? Are you thinking about what happened?"

Jordan was taken aback, "What?" Dr. Wright did not have Evelyn's gift of perception. And why would she just assume that she was thinking about that? How rude! And to just ask about it!

"Well you looked like you were in pain, so I just thought that maybe you were thinking about what had happened. It was traumatic and nobody would blame you if that was all you thought about!" Dr. Wright explained.

Jordan didn't know what to think, "I told you; I don't want to think about it."

"I understand that you don't want to think about it, but it is kind of hard not to, isn't it?" Dr. Wright inquired.

"No it isn't, I don't want to and I already told you that." Jordan stately frankly.

"Ok. Well, did you happen to think about the things I talked about yesterday?"

"No. That goes in the category of I don't want to talk about it or think about it!" Jordan stated "And I would like you to leave."

Dr. Wright took a deep breath and closed her notebook. "I understand that you are upset. I will come back later." She got up and walked out.

Jordan couldn't put her finger on it, but something bothered her about Dr. Wright.

TWENTY-NINE

Kate knocked on the hospital door. "Hey girl! How are you holding up?"

Jordan looked away from the TV to the door at the very familiar voice that she had missed. She smiled at her and said "Gosh I missed you!"

"I missed you too!" She grabbed her hand and held it. "I'm not asking what happened, but are you ok?"

"I don't know. But I think I will be one day. Just don't know when that will be." Jordan said.

"Well I am here for you whatever you need, whenever you need it! Got it? All you have to do is call!"

Kate got her all caught up on the things that have been happening, they talked for forever. They had been chatting for a long time, and the thought that kept coming up in Jordan's mind was how long have I been gone for? Nobody had said and she was almost afraid to ask. But she knew who she could ask.

Later that night, Evelyn came in to check on her. "How are you doin' darling?"

"I have been waiting for you. I have a question for you." Jordan stated flatly.

"Oh you do, do you?" Evelyn replied with a raised eyebrow.

Jordan took a deep breath, "I need to know how long I was gone."

Evelyn didn't look startled by the question, as usual, it was like she was expecting it. "Well, it was four weeks and four days." Jordan took in the information. She knew it had been a long time, but four weeks!! She had no idea that it had been that long. The thought of it almost took her breath away. Of course, Evelyn was right there; "take a deep breath, it's ok! Don't you worry. Everything is ok now."

Jordan hadn't really thought much about it. But now it felt like a lifetime had passed in those four weeks. She was suddenly so angry that those four weeks had been taken from her. She thought about all the things Kate had told her had happened and that she had missed and she was so angry. Evelyn gave her a hug, "It's ok, it's ok dear! I know you are angry and hurt and so many other feelings that you just don't even have a name for yet. But it is going to be ok! God is going to get you through this. You feel his peace over you. It is going to get better."

"Why did they do this to me? Why me?? I am so angry that they took this time from me! It was my time! It wasn't theirs to take!" Jordan sobbed.

"You are right. It was your time. And I don't know what God has in store for your life, but I guarantee that he has such an amazing plan for your life!" Evelyn told her.

"How do you have such faith that everything is going to be fine?" Jordan asked her.

"God gives us faith for the tough times. Have you ever heard the Lord's prayer?" Evelyn asked her.

"Yea I suppose so." Jordan replied while sniffling.

"Well," said Evelyn, pulling up a seat on Jordan's bed, "it says, 'Yea, though I walk through the valley of the shadow of death'. It doesn't say "IF" I walk or "MAYBE I will walk". God is telling us that we will have rough times, but he is with us, Always. Now I know that rough times is an understatement for what you are going through, but he was with you every minute."

"Why didn't he save me then?" Evelyn also seemed to know that question was coming too, so she settled herself in on Jordans bed.

"God gave man free will. And unfortunately, some choose to do bad things. I guess that is the simplest of explanations that there is. There isn't an easy answer to that question. But sometimes the devil leads people the wrong way and doing the wrong things. And the best we can do is follow God's plan after those things happen and see what he does with it. I haven't told many people around here this; but I lost my son a few years back. He was 16, coming home from a winning football game and was hit by a drunk driver. I was devastated. He was my world. I was very angry with God for quite some time. But I have worked through that, and although I don't know why God couldn't have made that car not start or make that drunk driver stumble and trip before getting into that car and save my son, he has shown me that I can do great things to help other people."

"I am sorry about your son." Jordan said and gave Evelyn a hug.

"See there dear, after everything you have been through, you still have such a big heart for Love and compassion, even in your time of pain. I am telling you that God has big plans for your life. You just watch and see!" Eveleyn said with a wink!

Thirty

"Well Jordan, it looks like we are ready to discharge you in the morning. We are going to give you some instructions for your injuries and how to take care of them at home. But we do need to talk about something. There is one test that we ran with your blood work and we need to discuss the results."

"I thought we went over all the results. Dr. James, I don't know what else there is to talk about. I am ready to go home." Jordan said with a moment of hesitation.

Dr. James pulled up a seat on her bed. "Jordan, I know that you don't want to talk about what happened, and that isn't what I am doing here. But we have to talk about the repercussions of what happened at the compound."

"Is that what they are calling it?" Jordan asked somewhat startled.

Dr. James took a deep breath. "The media has gotten a hold of the story. Fifteen girls from all over the country were found in a building and forced to fight and be slaves of the night to whoever has the highest bid. The building was massive, so they have dubbed it 'the compound."

"Oh. I didn't know that there were so many girls." Jordan said, looking down and fidgeting with her hands.

"Jordan, here is the deal. You don't have to tell me what happened there. I can tell, I am a doctor. So when you came in, we tested you for sexually transmitted diseases and we did a pregnancy test." He said, looking at her very gently. Jordan felt like she could be knocked over with a feather. In all of that apparent four weeks, pregnancy and STD's were not something that had ever crossed her mind. "Jordan, your STD results were all fine." She felt a huge sigh of relief. But as soon as it was out, she was overcome with panic. She looked up at the doctor with fear all over her face. He placed his hand on hers. "Jordan, I am so sorry; your pregnancy test was positive." She started to cry. All of a sudden, Evelyn was at her side hugging her and telling her it was going to be ok. Jordan sobbed uncontrollably. The doctor gave Evelyn a nod and she nodded back saying that she had control of the situation.

She stayed for hours holding Jordan. She finally had her asleep and went to the cafeteria to get her some food for when she woke up. Dr. Wright came in and shook Jordan awake. "Hey, I am so sorry to hear the news. How are you doing?"

"I don't know." Jordan said, sitting up and sniffling.

"Well I wanted to stop in and see how you are doing and talk to you about your options." Dr. Wright said. Jordan fidgeted and didn't know what to say. "Jordan, you do have options. You don't have to carry this to term and look at it every day, knowing where it came from, you can terminate the pregnancy." Jordan looked startled at the thought.

"You need to leave right now!" Evelyn stormed into the room. "You have no right to be in here right now talking about this. She just found out that she is having a baby, you have no right to tell her to get rid of it." Jordan was shocked. She was shocked that the doctor had just advocated for an abortion, and even more shocked that Evelyn was mad. Not even regular person mad, but fuming mad! She didn't know what to say, so she just sat there and watched the fight, astonished.

"She doesn't have to do this. She doesn't have to have this baby. She can just go back to the way things were before she was kidnapped. She can start her life fresh!" Dr. Wright said who was also mad! But she was no match for Evelyn.

"Every baby is a gift from God! She does not have to kill this baby. She has been given the gift of love and compassion and forgiveness. She can look into that precious baby's eyes and know that God gave her a gift and she can use that gift to give this child life and love and she can find forgiveness and be able to move forward." Evelyn said.

"Please! It isn't even a baby yet. And every time she looks at it, she will replay what happened." Dr. Wright scoffed.

"You need to leave now." Evelyn stated in the whisper that only parents use when they are about to lose their minds. Dr. Wright gave her a long hard stare and then stalked out. Evelyn looked upwards towards heaven and a few seconds later, she looked at Jordan who was wide eyed and staring at her. "I am sorry about that. She shouldn't be talking to you about that."

"You disagree with her." She said it as more of a question than a statement.

Evelyn took a deep breath and put the pudding and spoon she had been holding onto the bedside table. "I believe that every life is a gift from God. And he can do amazing things with people and he has a plan for every life. He can take some of the most horrible things and make them into something beautiful, and I believe that is what he is doing here. He has given you a gift, something beautiful that you can use to move forward."

"How do I move forward? What if she is right and everytime I look at the baby I see what happened?" Jordan asked.

"It is absolutely possible, for a while. But God can heal anything, and you never know what can happen when you hold that precious baby in your arms. You may look at that baby and see your whole future unfold. Babies can heal the brokest of hearts. And maybe this is God's way of helping you to see something else when you close your eyes." Evelyn said.

"My head is spinning. I don't know what to think." Jordan said, rubbing her forehead.

"Well, they are springing you from this joint tomorrow. What do you say to going to church with me tomorrow, maybe that will help." Evelyn said.

Jordan looked up, surprised at the invitation. "I've never been to church before." She felt nervous about going.

"Honey, that's ok. My church is very laid back and casual. Most people wear jeans and a t-shirt. And you don't need to know anything or do any studying, just show up." Evelyn stated.

"Umm… yea I guess so. I feel like I can't just really go back to my old life." Jordan said.

"Ok, church starts at 8:30, so I will pick you up at 7:30 and we can get your things loaded up and I can drop you at home afterwards." Evelyn planned. Jordan nodded and smiled.

Thirty-one

In the morning, Jordan was up and getting her things together. She couldn't believe how she had come there with nothing, and through the visits and flowers and gifts, she had so much stuff. She didn't know where she was going to put it all. She heard someone behind her.

"Jordan, I just wanted to talk to you after last night." Dr. Wright stated.

"Look, I went to health class in high school. I am aware of all of the options and what is available to me in these situations. I don't need to be advised." Jordan informed her.

Dr. Wright sat down. "Jordan, I have worked with so many people in your situation, and people who have gone through what you are going through. And I need you to trust me when I say that you will regret going through with this."

"For a shrink, I find your statement very interesting." Jordan stated. Dr. Wright cocked her head to the side in question of what she meant. "Well I thought that you were supposed to help me work through my feelings and not dictate them to me. Just because that is your experience in the past, doesn't mean that will be mine. And you don't know me. So how could you possible know how I would feel in this situation?"

"Jordan..." Dr. Wright started to speak but was cut off.

"I would like you to leave." Jordan stood straight up in front of her and looked her square in the eye when she said it so she would know how serious she was.

Dr. Wright stood up, straightening her skirt and left. Jordan smiled at herself for her ability to stand up to her. She didn't think that she would have it in her to tell her to leave.

She stuffed more stuff in a bag, and it felt like someone was watching her. She looked up, startled. "I didn't mean to make you jump, I'm sorry!" Mike said, holding his hand up in an offer of peace.

Jordan took a deep breath, "It's ok!"

He was hesitant to move forward anymore. So he stayed where he was, terrified that he was going to scare her again. "Umm I heard you were getting out today, so I thought I would give you a ride home."

"Oh thanks, but I... um am going to... somewhere with someone first." Jordan stammered it out, she didn't really know what to say. She felt awkward talking to him. He hadn't really visited. But it wasn't that. She just felt like she wasn't the same person that she was before. Like she had to get to know him all over again.

"Oh, I didn't know you would have plans." Now they both felt awkward.

"Hey look I'm sorry, I didn't know you would be here." Jordan stumbled. She hesitated, "look, why don't you come with me? I am sure that Evelyn wouldn't mind. If you want to."

He looked at her questioningly, "Where are you going?"

She smiled, "Evelyn has been helping me through some things, and so she invited me to... church." She waited for him to laugh at her.

But he wasn't laughing. "Jordan, I don't know what happened to you. But I know that you obviously have some things to figure out. But the one thing that I have learned from this is that I don't want one more day to go by without telling you something." He was looking her right in eye and he never even hinted at laughing at her. But he stepped closer to her. "I need you to know..." He was interrupted when Evelyn walked in the room.

"Well, are you ready to go? Oh so sorry, I didn't know you had a visitor, I wouldn't have barged in." Evelyn said. "Let me just take this to the car, and then we can go. Are WE going?" Evelyn asked, looking at Mike. Evelyn raised an eyebrow.

Mike looked at Jordan, "I will go anywhere you go." He stated looking at her. Jordan looked at him with all of the bruising on her face, and she felt that he was looking right through them to her soul. There was the friend she knew and loved. And with that, Mike leaned over and picked up some stuff and started to walk out, pausing to wait for Jordan. Evelyn looked at him and gave him a goofy sort of smile and laughed.

Thirty-two

They all piled into Evelyn's car. "So hi, I'm Mike. I haven't met you yet." Evelyn smiled at him.

"It is so very nice to meet you!" Evelyn said. "I am super glad that you decided to come with us! So have you ever been to church?"

He smiled back at her timidly, "um no I haven't. So do you want to clue us in to what we are in for here?"

She laughed, "Well there will be no sacrificing chickens or anything if that is what you are wondering."

Mike and Jordan laughed too. "Well that helps." Mike said.

"Ok. So we start with worship. It isn't like hymns or anything like that. There is a band, and some of them are upbeat songs with a drummer and guitars."

"Sounds like a concert, not church." Mike said.

"Well the times have changed and we are changing with it. Church is fun these days. Modern music and then the pastor gives up and gives his message."

"Well that doesn't sound too painful." Mike joked and Jordan smiled.

"It is a very fun and peaceful time." Evelyn said. She looked so peaceful just thinking about it. They arrived and she parked and they got out and started to walk in. Jordan thought that she would feel anxious and nervous about going. Worried that people would stare at her because of the bruises and talk in hushed voices about her or what happened. But she didn't feel the nervousness or anxiety at all. People looked at her and smiled and went on about their business.

They found seats in the sanctuary. Jordan noticed that this wasn't like what she had thought it would be like. She didn't see pews or hymnals. There were chairs and she could see a drum set on the stage and guitars and a keyboard. She wondered what the music would be like. The first song when the band got up there was something that started 'Let everything that has breath.' This church was rocking! People were clapping and singing. Jordan smiled and thought it was pretty cool! The next song was called 'Waymaker' but it was the last one that really stuck with her, it was called 'There's another in the Fire.' For some reason, she felt this song deep inside of her, and it took her breath away. It was at that moment that she realized that it had been Jesus who was with her in that ring. He put himself inbetween her and the punches and saved her from the beating that the doctor kept telling her she should have had. She couldn't believe that he had been with her, but at the same time, she knew it and she felt it, he was with her.

The pastor got up on stage and welcomed everyone. They all sat down. "Good morning church! We have a heavy topic for today. So I want you all to prepare yourselves. If you need to get up and leave, that is ok too, I won't be offended. I want to talk about forgiveness. And I know you are saying 'oh that's easy.' But what about when it isn't little things that we need to forgive? Let me ask you this question. Don't worry, it's fill in the blanks. You don't have to say it out loud, but be honest with yourself. How many of you have said this statement… If 'blank' happened to me, I would never forgive that person? If my spouse cheated on me, we would be divorced! If anyone ever hurts my kids, I would never forgive them. All of these things are saying that you choose not to forgive. You choose not to give to others what God has given to you. I know that some of you have been through some very rough times, and you needed to forgive someone. And sometimes you dug your heels in, because you were hurt, and you didn't want to forgive them because you are still hurt. 'I can't forgive them, I am still hurting.' I hear that statement a lot. But…." He emphasized this word, "But! We have to remember that healing the hurt comes after forgiveness. Forgiveness isn't easy. It is easy to let the devil split your family, or hold a grudge, and never make amends with someone. Being a Christian isn't easy. We have tough times because the devil tries to tear us down. But with faith comes forgiveness. With forgiveness comes healing. With healing and forgiveness comes freedom. I don't know what you are going through, but I know that some of you need to have a conversation with God and talk about forgiveness."

Jordan was listening intently. She felt excited about what he was saying. She wanted healing, and freedom. But does that mean that she has to forgive Elijah for everything that happened? She wasn't sure that she could do that. How do you forgive someone for taking your childhood and subjecting her to the horrors of what happened to her? She listened to the pastor as he recited some scriptures which she didn't recognize, and felt like she wanted more. More of the peace and understanding that Evelyn has. But could she have that after what she went through, and what she was facing with this baby? Oh God, the baby. Would God forgive her if she chose to have an abortion like Dr. Wright was suggesting? Or like Evelyn said, could she have all the peace and healing that she says God will give to her? She was mulling over all of these questions and thoughts and didn't realize people were starting to stand up and go up to the altar and accept God into their lives. She didn't even realize that she was moving until she was up there with everyone else. She bowed her head and prayed the prayer after the pastor, "Lord God, come into my life and heal me and my broken heart. Help me forgive those who have trespassed against me. Lord give me guidance to live the life that you want me to live and walk down your path." She felt Evelyn's hand on her back. Jordan turned around and smiled at her and they hugged.

Evelyn introduced her to some people on the way out and she shook hands and smiled and Mike was there with her. They got to the car, and all the car doors closed and Evelyn looked at Mike and said "Well what do you think?"

Mike kinda shrugged. "It sounds good, but forgiveness isn't just that easy. Some things are just too hard to forgive."

"Like forgiving a drunk driver for killing your son?" Evelyn said quietly. Mike looked at her wide eyed and took the hint and was quiet. "It is hard, and there isn't a day that goes by that I don't think about that day. But forgiveness is the lock and key to my freedom to be free from that day and not live it over and over and over again in my mind. I will not be a slave to it."

Jordan looked at her astonished. That is exactly what she wanted. To not be a slave to that time anymore. She just didn't know how to do it, even though she had taken that step and accepted Jesus into her life, what was she supposed to do next?

Thirty-three

Evelyn dropped her off at her house, and Mike said he would catch up with her later. He asked Evelyn to drop him off at his car. Jordan walked up to her house. It felt like forever since she had been there. Her dad came out to meet her. "Hey dear. Sorry I didn't visit you more, I just thought maybe you were better off without me in your way."

"Thanks dad. It's ok. I appreciate the space." She smiled and gave him a hug and they walked in the house. They put her things away and her dad stood there awkwardly. "Dad thanks for everything, but I'm ok. I'm gonna take a nap I think."

"Ok. Well let me know if you need anything. I will be downstairs." He stepped forward and gave her an awkward light hug and then left.

Jordan felt awkward being back at home again. Her thoughts were all over the place. Being back at home. Feeling weird around everyone because she didn't feel like herself anymore. She felt like a different person. She just couldn't seem to wrap her head around everything that had happened since the time that she had been abducted. How could all of that happen? The abduction, the training, the fights, the rescue… and all ending with the baby. The baby. What the heck about that? What to do about that? She felt cooped up, and so she got up and went outside for a walk. As she got outside, Mike drove up and asked her if he could go with her.

"I don't think that you should be walking around alone." Mike told her.

"Well I can't be watched forever." She told him.

"I understand. I just think that since it sounds like they didn't get the head guy who was in charge of it all, that maybe you don't need to be alone until he is found." Mike said, seeming nonchalant.

Jordan stopped dead in her tracks and slowly looked up at him. "What?"

Mike stopped and turned around not realizing that she had stopped. "What? One of the other girls that was found, gave a statement to the police and looked at pictures and said that the head guy wasn't in the photos of people that had been arrested. Nobody told you?"

"We have to go to the police station right now." Jordan said, rushing back to Mike's car who seemed utterly confused but he jumped in and started driving her to the police station. She seemed jumpy and agitated all of a sudden.

They got there and Mike barely had time to put the car in park before she jumped out and ran inside. "I need to speak to the person in charge of the case where all the girls were found." She told the police woman at the front desk.

"Sure. Have a seat." She said calmly. She picked up the phone and made a call. Jordan didn't sit down, but she just paced in front of some chairs.

A couple minutes later a cop came out and called her by her name. Normally she would have thought that was odd, but this time she decided that it didn't matter. "Jordan, I am Detective Scott, how can I help you?"

"I need to see the pictures of all the people that you arrested, it's important!" she said breathlessly. She felt like her worst nightmare was coming to life. She thought that everything was ok, but she had never thought that he wouldn't have been caught.

"Ok, let's go take a look." He led her and Mike back through a door to his desk and grabbed a folder. "Ok, this is a picture of everyone that was arrested. And this one is all the victims that were found." And then he handed her a second folder.

She started hastily looking through the first folder. "They are not here." She looked down and put her hand on her forehead and started crying. The detective and Mike looked bewildered. They had no idea who "they" were, but clearly this was devastating news.

"Umm… Jordan," the detective approached her with a tissue like she was a bomb that was about to go off. "Who are 'they?'"

She sniffed and the tears were still rolling. And she started talking. "Elijah and Mace. Elijah was the head of all of it. He raped girls and forced them to fight, and then the spectators would bid on the winner and they would get to spend the night with her and do anything that they wanted. Beat, rape, anything. Mace was a trainer. He was my trainer. He knew the other girls and he would give me advice on how to win. I didn't know what happened to the winners at the time, but Mace told me it was better than losing."

Detective Scott looked like he could be knocked over with a feather and Mike looked positively ill. Jordan didn't look up. She knew if she saw Mike's face that she wouldn't be able to continue and she needed the detective to know how terrible Elijah was so he could find him. "Jordan, did Elijah ever rape you?" he asked with hesitation.

"Yes." She said looking right at Mike. She realized that if she didn't have the guts to look him in the eye right then, then she never would.

"Often?" The detective asked.

"When I woke up, I was groggy and I think that he drugged me, but he was there in the room with me and that was the first time. Then when I won that first fight, he beat me and raped me." Jordan said.

"And this trainer Mace? Did he ever rape you?" the detective asked.

"No. I think that he was actually being held captive in a way as well. He has a kid, and Elijah was keeping them apart and threatening to kill him if he didn't train the girls." She stated.

"Do you have any idea where they might go?" He asked.

"No, but I think that Mace knew that something was going to happen." She thought, she was startled by the thought, because it just dawned on her.

"What do you mean?" the detective asked.

"Well I didn't realize it until just now. But Mace trained me almost everyday except that day, but another trainer came and got me and told me that Mace said if anything happened, then to get down and stay down. But I never saw Mace that day." She remembered.

The detective leaned back in his chair and rubbed his chin. He took a huffy breath and leaned back forwards toward Jordan. "Look, would you recognize this Mace guy's voice if you heard it?"

She nodded "I think so. Why?"

He hesitated, looking between the two of them. "Look, this hasn't been released yet, and nobody other than select officers knows this. We received a tip on the emergency line, and that is how we found you girls. From what you are saying, I think maybe it was him."

He pulled up a file on his computer and hit play. "There is a warehouse on highway ninety-eight, you will find all of the missing girls there. The person in charge is Elijah Woods." And then he hung up.

Tears filled her eyes again, "that's Mace." She confirmed for the detective.

"Thank you Jordan. I know that this must've been terrible for you." the detective said and he actually looked really sad.

"So what do I do now, since he is still out there?" Jordan asked.

"Well there is no telling that he won't try something, but there isn't anything saying that he hasn't run for the hills either. So we will be taking the side of caution and putting a detective with you at all times." the detective stated. "This is detective Randall. He goes where you go. You pee, he pees. You go to class, he goes to class." She nodded. "Just let me know if you think of anything else that might help us find them. You have been extremely helpful." She got up and moved towards the door with Mike. "And Jordan.. I am sorry that you had to go through all of this."

Jordan turned back, "You found the doctor, his picture is in there. Can I talk to him?"

Mike was astonished. "Jordan, you can't be serious?"

"I am serious. I think that like Mace, he wasn't there by choice. He was nice to me. He tried to help me."

The detective was watching this exchange, and he finally spoke up. "Jordan, I agree with you. Doctor Woods was captured and I wish I could help him but he won't give us anything. Maybe you can help me."

"What do you mean? How can I help?" Jordan asked.

"Well you want to talk to him, so talk. But what I need to know is any inside information that he may have about where Elijah might have gone." He said all of this while walking her to a cell in the back of the building through many doors. "Here you go. Doctor, you have a visitor." He said clanking the keys on the cell.

The doctor sat up. He looked at Jordan and smiled. "You are ok. Although I don't know why I am surprised, you always were. So are you ready to tell me how you avoided so many injuries?"

"Why do you keep asking about that?" Jordan understood being curious, but he just wouldn't give it up.

He took a deep breath and sat on a bench next to the cell door. "Jordan, I am going to tell you something, and you might think that I am crazy. I was there by chance, and yet by choice. I had a big gambling debt and I owed Elijah a lot of money. He agreed to settle the debt if I were to be a doctor on his service. I didn't know that meant servitude and isolation. Although, as I began to pray about it, God told me that I was there for a reason. To help look after the girls, and a little boy. Keep them safe and help them. I know that God saved you from injuries during that fight. There is no way that you could have sustained the very few injuries that you did without the intervention of the lord."

Jordan hung on every word that he said. "Wait, a little boy? What was his name?"

Dr. Woods was rubbing his chest. "His name was Samuel. Elijah was keeping him from Mace. He told me that if I told Mace about him and where he was, that he would kill Sam. Sam is a wonderful little guy. Elijah is a very bad man, and I wanted to keep the boy, and you girls as safe as I possibly could." He looked up at her and said, "Jordan, I am so sorry." He rubbed his chest more and looked out of breath.

"Dr. are you ok? You don't look well." He was sweating and red in the face. He started to fall over. "Guard!! We need help!"

"Jordan," he said breathlessly, "find his cabin!" And then he slumped.

"Doctor!" Jordan screamed! Guards came rushing and opened the door and she fell on her knees crying as they began to perform CPR on him. Mike was behind her hugging her.

Thirty-four

A week later, Mike and Jordan were getting ready for church. Jordan was still upset about Doctor Woods. The detective told her that he died of a heart attack. She had spoken with Evelyn and told her about the doctor. Evelyn, like everything else, seemed unphased that he was there trying to help.

They had roped Kate into going with them. Kate seemed intrigued. Her parents weren't church goers, but it wasn't like they didn't believe in God. The three kids met Evelyn in the parking lot and went in and found seats. The worship and sermon spoke volumes to Jordan. She was ready to move on to forgiveness and something new.

They left and as they were walking out, Mike asked Jordan if they could take a walk later. She agreed and reminded him that she had a shadow, so it would have to be the three musketeers on a walk. They dropped off Kate and went on a walk around the lake.

"Jordan, there is something I have been trying to tell you since the day you were abducted. And I need to tell you before anything else happens." Mike said and it wasn't like it was hot out, but he was kinda sweating.

"What's up?" Jordan asked.

"That day when I kissed you, I didn't mean to. I wanted to talk to you, but I couldn't find the words. But now, if I don't tell you, I just might die." Mike said.

"Mike, you are starting to kind of freak me out a bit." Jordan said.

"Jordan, I love you. I have been in love with you forever. And it killed me when I couldn't help you. And it kills me knowing that that guy's hands were on you. But I want to put my hands on his throat and wait until every breath leaves his soul to let go. I know that goes against what that pastor says, but I can't help feeling that." Mike poured his soul out to her.

"Well here is your opportunity to do just that, noble boyfriend." That voice was like ice going down her back, and she felt it before she saw him. She knew who it was. Mike whipped around to face him and he blocked Jordan from his view.

Jordan felt this overwhelming sense of getting herself back and she stepped out in front of Mike and looked Elijah square in the eye. "The police are looking for you. I have security, and he will see you and catch you and you will go to trial for all that you did."

"Oh I don't think that will be happening any time soon. Where is your security detail by the way?" He said looking around, "Seems to have disappeared. Well anyways, I don't think that you realize how far my reach goes. I think that you need to realize that you are mine, and you will always be mine." He said, reaching out and moving a piece of hair off her forehead. She jerked away from him. "Besides, we are forever linked now." He said, raising his eyebrow at her. "It is true what they say, you are truly glowing!"

Mike seemed to catch on that there was something he was missing, and he thought that he knew what it was but still wanted to hear it to know that it was real. "Jordan, what is he talking about?"

"Oh, you haven't told the illustrious boyfriend yet? Does he know that you talk in your sleep? 'I love you Mike, don't leave me Mike." he said in a sing-song voice. "Well, at some point, he is going to realize when you start packing on the weight, you know in the tummy area. Well don't you worry, I will be back before the little bundle arrives. Lord knows that I can't wait to be a daddy." And with that, Elijah walked off.

Mike's head was reeling. And Jordan was freaking out! Where was the cop? Why didn't he see him? Oh my god, was he going to take her baby?

They watched him get into the black SUV and leave. Jordan whipped around.

"Oh my god. Ok, Mike first of all, yes I am pregnant. Yes it is Elijah's. No one else touched me while I was gone. I don't know what I am going to do." And then she looked straight at him, "and yes, I love you too!"

If it was possible for his head to explode, then now would've been it. Before he could say anything, she jumped in again. "Look, you don't have to say anything. It's fine. We all need time to sort things out."

"Marry me?" He said, looking straight at her.

"What?" she said stepping back thinking that a step's distance would help her understand those two words that he just said.

"Marry me? I know it sounds crazy, and we are only sixteen. But I love you, and I will never love anyone else like you. And I want to help you heal. And whatever happens with this baby, we will be a family and I will never let that man hurt you or the baby. I swear I will protect you with my life." He professed his love to her as he reached out and grabbed her hand.

Tears streamed down her face, and she looked up into his eyes and she was so confused and had no idea what to do next.

About the Author

Trista is a Christian mom of 5 kids. She believes that God has called her to help teens navigate the difficulties of being a godly teenager in today's culture. She hopes to reach people on their level and help keep them on the path of righteousness.

Printed in the United States
by Baker & Taylor Publisher Services